Copyright © 2024 by Ian Fanselow



Book Cover by Candice Broersma

Illustrations by Candice Broersma and Jessica Cvilo

1st edition 2024

# ACKNOWLEDGMENTS

This story went through quite a journey to get from me to you. Some of those steps are obvious, like the book being shipped to you or finding it in a library or bookstore. Many more steps, however, may not be so obvious. I would like to use this page to illuminate those steps and the people who were pivotal in them.

First, the book in your hands is draft 12.4, and much of the quality of this story comes from the iterations that came before. Those iterations were motivated by people who were willing to read this story in a state far inferior to what you hold now.

Those people are: Jessica Gulack, Brandt Weary, Sumner Schwartz, Tommy Molloy, Michael Cordista, Eirik Humlen, Daria Black, Barbara Knowlton, Michael Fanselow, Rich Cooper, Emily Tran, Erin Hassman, Theresa Brown, Keira Kamath, Isabella Tan, Jiya Sandhu, Kingston Harrison, Willie Tsai, Ali Farzhad, Jeanne Robert-Huet, Kiyan Zamani, Yogesh Dhamija, and Elaine Abrams. These people all had to bear me asking countless questions about their thoughts on every detail and did so all out of friendship. Remove any name from this list, and the book would be lesser.

I also would like to thank a few professionals, who's work improved the book greatly. Mary Kole, who helped me find Lora's interiority and insisted upon its presence in every moment. If you heard about this book from anywhere other than me directly, it is likely due to the diligent plans of Heather Wallace. If you read a paragraph and notice no grammatical errors, please thank Alexandra Ott, because I certainly do not deserve the credit for that. P. J. Hoover polished down every crack that interrupted the flow of the story and helped each scene focus on the right tone. Candice Broersma created the beautiful cover and chapter illustrations, from the moment I got the final version of the cover art I have proudly shown it to every person I can as though I were a new parent and it were a picture of my child. The chapter headings and overall design of the book you hold were created by Jessica Cvilo as well as the art for the spotlight chapter.

While it may be my name on the cover, these 29 people were pivotal in making the experience of reading this book something I can be proud of.

# WORLDS APART

**Prediction Engine At 80%.**

Fydlon stares at the giant screen displaying statistics in bright green symbols. They built the most powerful machine in the entire galaxy, hidden away deep in the space between stars. Only two others in the universe know its location, but all they can get is 80%. Arwein is right; they need the girl.

Conquering Earth would be easy for Fydlon. Their primitive weapons would have little effect on his stonelike skin, and his strength and stature far exceed anything the earthlings could comprehend. After all, he has commanded armies larger than the population of the planet, but this plan requires secrecy. After inputting the coordinates for Earth, he soars away from the station in the darkest part of the galaxy, traveling alone to capture the human.

# CHAPTER 1

# LORA, THE HUMAN

**"WILL YOU GO TO THE GRADUATION DANCE WITH ME?"** I ask. *No, that doesn't sound right. It's too uncool.* Okay, how about just saying "the dance"? Everyone knows which one I mean, right?

"Mrrow," Button responds. The cat struts along the desk as if I am not currently going through a major crisis. She can be a very unhelpful cat at times. Instead, I look for non-feline encouragement elsewhere in my room. Heroes of science-fiction movies from before I was born stare down at me from their posters. What would they do? *They'd know how to ask without being the most awkward thing on the planet.* I need to rehearse more.

"So... how 'bout that dance? You got a date yet? No? Me neither, why don't... no, no, no, that's stupid." Maybe today is not— *No! It has to be today; you made the plan.* Right, It's the last dance before high school. The internet said two weeks before is the optimal time to ask.

"Meow." Button investigates the small car made from a shoebox colored with blue and green flames.

"No, Button, not that one." I rescue the homemade vehicle from curious claws and take a minute to trace the elegant swirls of painted fire with my eyes. *You have a mission.* Right, I lay the small car down in a more Button-proof place. Disappointed there are no more prized possessions to ruin, she hops down onto the rug that shows every planet in the solar system.

"Lora, we should get going!" Mom calls from downstairs.

"Be right there." I grab my phone off the charger.

## 3:27 p.m. May 4th, four bars of reception, 98% battery

I can do this. I can do this. What's the worst that could happen? *Do you want a list of all the worst possibilities?* After a deep breath, I give one more pet to Button below the bright blue chrysanthemum flower that fastens her collar. Then I grab my backpack and do one last outfit check.

Olive-green jeans and a simple patterned white-and-black shirt with just a little asymmetry flowing at the bottom. This outfit statistically, has gotten the most compliments, even after filtering out potentially sarcastic ones. *You need the sweater.* Right, my lucky green knit sweater. It may not actually be lucky, but I have gotten an A on every test I took while wearing it, and I was wearing it last year when I won the Voyage Con tickets. Superstition or not, this isn't a day to leave anything to chance. *Now just stick to the plan.*

"We're leaving in one minute," Mom calls again.

I pull the sweater over my head while rushing down the stairs to the living room. Before Mom opens the door to leave, Dad pops his head out of the kitchen. "Hey, wait up! Check this out before you go."

I look to Mom for permission. "Be quick," she says.

Inside the kitchen, Dad is stirring two pots at the same time. "I made you a snack. New recipe." With his hands occupied, he gestures with his head towards a small Tupperware container. Inside are three carefully arranged dumplings.

"There's food at the festival," I say. "I'm gonna eat that."

"I know, but just in case. Also thought I'd let my guinea pig try it before bringing it to the restaurant."

"Ah, so there's ulterior motives," I joke.

He lets go of the two wooden spoons and raises his hands in surrender. "You caught me."

"Lora," Mom calls from the other room. "We should get going." I take the Tupperware and wave goodbye to Dad as I head to the car.

Opening the passenger door pulls the smells of Thai food and fake leather into the air. I perch my legs up as I sit to avoid stepping in week-old takeout boxes that litter the floor of the passenger seat. After a few minutes of quietly driving towards the school, Mom breaks the silence.

"Make sure to attach the ground wire."

"What?" I ask.

"At the festival, when you set up. Attach the ground wire before anything else."

"Yes, Mom, I remember."

"And also wear the gloves when you're—"

"I remember." I said that too forcefully, or at least I think I did. Silence pours into the car, and Mom shifts in her seat.

"So, um, great! What time should I pick you up?" Mom says.

"I don't know," I say. I can't think about this now; I have to concentrate. *Rehearse it again.*

"Well, the festival is supposed to go until ten. Will you stay the whole—"

"I don't know." I run my fingers through my hair.

"I'm letting you be independent; you can decide how long to stay. I just need to know when to drive back. That's a lot more freedom than my parents ever gave me."

I've heard this a thousand times already.

"I didn't even say anything when you dyed your hair, so I think—"

"Saying 'I didn't say anything about it' counts as saying something," I interject. "And auburn is a normal color."

Silence drowns the car, but that's okay, because I'm right. Auburn is a normal color, and I am thirteen. I can dye my hair if I want to. *This isn't important now.*

"So... Lora."

"So... Mom."

"I just mean, you know, you can talk to me about anything, right?" Mom starts. "We used to talk all the time."

"I know."

"Like, this morning, when you were in your room, I overheard—"

"Mom! You were spying on me?" I should've had music playing to drown out the sound. *Just ignore it, a messy heart-to-heart with Mom is not part of the plan.* I look out the window, trying to count the streets we pass.

My arms and legs start to feel like worms, constantly wiggling

without moving anywhere, as I slide down in my seat.

"Now, who were you planning to ask?" Mom questions.

"It's not important."

"Come on! What's his name? Do I know him?"

"Mom, stop!" I yell. Immediately, I feel sick. I shouldn't yell like that; I'm a teenager now, not a little kid. But why does Mom have to interrogate me! *Whatever, just don't let this distract you from what's import-ant.* Right, I take all the anxiety from talking to Mom and pack it in a little box. Then I take that box and place it neatly in a pile labeled "deal with later"... That's better.

"I... I'll tell you about it tonight. I'm sorry," I say as I unbuckle my seatbelt. That's right, after tonight I'll have fixed everything, and then there'll be time to figure out how to tell her.

"Ah, you will ask during the festival? Good choice."

I nod and slink out of the car.

"Have a good day. I love you," Mom says way too loudly.

What is she doing? Is she trying to embarrass me on purpose? I quickly check, but fortunately, no one is around. "Yeah, um, thanks for the ride."

Mom pulls her lips to a line and nods before driving away. Normally, going to school on a Saturday would suck. But today has the power to change everything. Nothing will be the same again. No matter what Evelyn says.

The only time I like being in the gym is at the Harthian Middle School yearly club festival. The courts transform into a vibrant maze of booths bursting with food, games, and anything to show off to the other students. Club presidents compete to have the most popular booth, sometimes planning for the entire next year. Of course, as the sci-fi club president, I planned mine three months ago. *Remember the plan.* Step one: assemble the sci-fi booth.

I start arranging the large pieces of cardboard I cut out last week. Slowly they begin to form the shape of a spaceship the size of a small room. Step two: set up all the wiring. Step three: with every-thing ready early, I can put my time in at the booth before sneaking away and—

"Lora!" a voice calls, breaking my concentration. I look up to see my best friend walking towards me. *She's early! That isn't the plan.* The bright gym lights normally bring out the worst looks, but not for Evelyn. Instead, her golden hair shimmers, framing her face in a warm glow. *The emergency exit for the gym is seventy-five feet away.* No, I don't need that. This is okay; the plan can still work.

"Sorry I'm a bit early," Evelyn starts. "It's a long drive for my mom, and she said she'd get home too late if she dropped me closer to six."

Why did Evelyn's mom have to move that far away? More importantly, why does she have to live with her? And all this without even asking me! Doesn't the best friend get some say in this? *Focus, you can fix this.*

"It's fine." It's not fine, but I can't just say that. This kind of problem needs a plan.

"Are you gonna spend the whole festival at your nerd booth?" Evelyn says playfully.

"Nah, I'll find a way to slip out, no problem." I said that in a cool way, right? Yeah, definitely.

"Good," Evelyn starts. "I was hoping we could hang. It'd probably suck without you."

My cheeks start to get warm.

"Okay, so," Evelyn says, looking at my hair. "Took me a few days to get used to it, but the new chestnut-maroon color suits you. Especially since you always wear greens." Evelyn gestures to my pants and sweater. "And I love this."

Does she mean me? Or the clothes? Or both? Or— *Breathe, she will see you blushing. Just act normal.*

"Thank you," I say, trying to smile just right. The friendship amount, instead of the crush-just-complimented-you-and-now-your-heart-is-melting amount.

The gym starts to get more and more crowded as the festival is about to start. Extravagant booths from every club slowly come together all around us.

Evelyn sighs. "You think they'll have stuff like this in high school?"

"Won't be the same without you." Did I just say that? Did I just give away how I feel? No, that's a normal friend thing to say. Definitely. After a moment, I notice Evelyn is gazing off with a distant look.

"Are you okay?" I ask.

"Me?" Evelyn quickly switches back to a smile. "Of course, dude. Two birthdays every year? It's gonna be great!" Evelyn's expression could fool most people, but not me. I've learned what each different smile she has means, and this one is not happy. "Okay, so, it's been, like, weeks since you invited me over!" Evelyn proclaims.

"Has it? I could've sworn you were—"

"And!" Evelyn interrupts. "That means it's been weeks since I've had your dad's cooking. How can I be deprived of such amazing food? It's a crime!" Evelyn pretends to faint dramatically, all while holding that same smile. The act draws a giggle out of me. *She's perfect.*

"You win. I'll let them know you'll come over."

The moment she sees me laughing, Evelyn's smile shifts to one I much prefer, a genuinely happy one. "Okay, so, I forgot to tell you!" Evelyn says. "My mom took me dress shopping this morning!"

"Dress shopping?"

"For the dance!"

Blood rushes to my face. *The emergency exit is seventy-five feet away.* Calm down. Seemingly ignorant of my imminent panic attack, Evelyn continues. "She made me promise to use it for every occasion through high school, but hey, I'll take what I can get. It's a gorgeous capri." She pauses for a moment. "Capri as in the color, not the style. It's like a beautiful deep azure blue."

*Matches your eyes.* No, don't say that, it's too obvious. But she knows I know what color her eyes are, so that's a normal thing to say.

"Anyway," Evelyn says. "It's super cute. I'll send you a pic. I'm sure you'd love it."

This is perfect, she brought up the dance so—*no, wait, this isn't the right time. Remember the plan, that has the highest chance of working. If this doesn't work she moves away, and you'll be all alone again.* Oh my gosh, she's looking at me, it's my turn to talk and I haven't said anything in too long.

"I, um, gotta get back to setting up the booth cause, um…" I mumble.

"Er, okay." Evelyn shrugs and leaves, giving me time to rush back to the half-constructed ship.

She can't move away. Evelyn's always been there, that's how it's supposed to be. *The emergency exit is sixty feet away.* My heart pounds, but I don't go for the exit. I can do this. I can feel tears forming, but I push them back. Crying is for when there's nothing left to do, and this plan is going to work. Step four: have the perfect night with Evelyn at the festival. Step five: ask her to the dance at the most perfect moment. Step six: have the best summer ever before Evelyn has to move. Step seven: we don't drift apart when we start different schools.

I repeat the plan a dozen times, until I don't feel like crying anymore. I almost messed it all up, and that is not an option. Stupid feelings, trying to ruin everything.

CHAPTER 2

# EARTH IS SMALL

**"YOU DIDN'T SET ANYTHING UP!"** squeals a voice, breaking my concentration. Even before looking, I already know who it is. Chester, the sci-fi club's vice president, is a mouseish boy who looks like he has the word "actually" tattooed on his forehead. He cycles through the same five outfits his mom picked out for him when he started middle school.

"I'm working on it." I hop out of the ship and clear up some scattered supplies on the floor. *He's right, you are behind, it should be almost done by now.*

"Is it even ready?" asks Chester without dropping his agitated tone. "You said you'd have it ready."

"Yeah, yeah, just hand me that screwdriver over there." I don't have time to get annoyed. *Just finish and get on with the plan.*

Chester obliges, handing me the screwdriver, and I start putting everything together. Chester only helps if I give him a specific instruction; otherwise he just stands around and makes comments. Eventually I stop trying and just let his complaints turn to background noise as I assemble the last few pieces of the cardboard starship. *You're forgetting the uniforms.* Right. I pull out a garbage bag from underneath the booth, filled with *Star Voyages* uniforms.

Chester looks inside. "I thought you were getting uniforms from the original. These are all from the second generation. Or don't you know the difference?"

"I prefer these."

"If you switched the uniforms, I assume—"

"Yes, Chester, I changed the bridge to match." I make a point of rolling my eyes. I know I'm not supposed to be confrontational today, since there are more important things to focus on. But one little eye roll never hurt anyone.

"Wish you ran it by me first. Also, you brought extra uniforms? We only need the two, and they look like all different sizes?"

"Better safe than sorry. Anyways, should be done now." I change the subject quickly and slot in the last pieces of the ship. Explaining the uniforms means explaining part of the plan, which leads to explaining the whole plan. The subject change worked, and we take a moment to marvel at what we, *mostly I,* built. A replica of the *Starship Expedition* from our favorite show, *Star Voyages.* The exterior of the ship is at one-fiftieth scale, making it about twenty feet long.

We walk up a staircase made from reinforced and painted cardboard boxes into the inside of the ship, which features a small room made from cardboard and Styrofoam. Chester feels around and presses a few buttons while I triple-check a half-dozen hidden speakers.

"It's perfect. An exact full-scale re-creation of the bridge," Chester says.

"Wait there. Let me show you the best part." I skip out of the room and hop down the stairs. Under the ship is a tangled mess of wires, and I follow one to the end. Once I plug it in, that's step two done: finish all the wiring. I suddenly freeze, my hand holding the wire shaking.

"Am I supposed to be seeing something?" Chester calls from inside the ship.

I'll have to ask her soon, it's getting closer, too close. *The exit is sixty-five feet away.* No, I can't run, I—

"I don't think you set it up right!" Chester yells.

I shake my head and tighten my grip around the wire until my hand stops shaking. I have a plan; following it is the only thing to do. I plug in the wire and call back to Chester. "My mom and I went over the specs together! She's literally an engineer." With that, I return to the bridge and slam a button.

Immediately, all the lights shut off and the buttons begin to blink. A voice booms from a hidden speaker, "Imperative! Imperative! This is the Calhoun Cruinn—nine units out of Aquila-Six. We have struck a gravity mine and have lost all power…"

"That's from…" Chester can hardly speak. He looks like he might even cry.

"I know, the second movie. If you press the buttons, it continues. The whole thing takes about five minutes, so I was thinking we let one in at a time, and they can be the captain," I explain. "My mom also set it up so you can choose how you respond in the situation. I had to use voice clips from the original show and second generation to do that. You don't mind, do you?"

Chester shakes his head slowly.

"I'll leave you alone for a minute. Come out when you're ready." With that done, I leave the bridge and return to the front of the booth. I hang a sign that reads *Become a Starship Captain!* and quickly check my phone.

## 5:01p.m., May 4th, two bars of reception, 94% battery.

T minus twenty-nine minutes. Need to put in some time here, then off to see Evelyn. This might actually work. I take a deep breath and survey the sci-fi club's competition. Next to my booth, the anime club advertises "Authentic Samurai Sword Lessons." *Seems dangerous.*

The debate club has a sign that reads, "We'll argue any topic you come up with." *That's gonna end poorly.*

The hip-hop club proudly displays "Dance battle tournament" along with a massive bracket of entrants. *Not the kind of dance to focus on today.*

Chester exits the ship in a blue uniform, clearly just having had an experience he's dreamed of for years.

"You want to try it out? There's probably time," Chester offers.

I shake my head. "Nah, no space adventures for me today. Anyways, the festival is gonna start soon. I'll get changed in the ship. Make sure no one comes in."

"Yes, captain," responds Chester with an official *Star Voyages* salute.

"At ease, Lieutenant Chester."

HARTHIAN
SCI-FI CLUB

As students flood into the gym, the rest of the sci-fi club arrives. They don't have to work the booth like Chester and I, but they all stop by to congratulate us on how the ship came out before moving on to other booths.

"Lora, you stay out there and guide people in," Chester says. "I'll run things from inside."

"Sure, that's fine."

Step 3: Find a way out of this. But I have to put in time here anyways. There's no reason I can't have the most popular booth *and* get a date to the dance. The sci-fi club president side of me takes over. I put a smile on my face, then let myself pretend to be in another galaxy.

Eventually, a boy approaches. "What's the deal with this one?" the boy asks.

"Welcome, captain!" I exclaim. "We have been called to a mission aboard the *Starship Expedition*. First Officer Chester is awaiting your command on the bridge!"

"…Okay." The boy shrugs and meanders up the stairs. Soon, the model ship blinks with LED lights accompanied by buzzes and whirs. I plug a microphone into a small amplifier and turn the volume dial until it stops at ten.

"We are in need of Starfleet captains! Will you answer the call?"

Most of the students appear confused, but the dazzling lights behind me seem to entice my classmates to check it out. Before long there is even a line to get in.

"Welcome, welcome! You all have the making of a great Starfleet captain, just step right up and—" I immediately break character as Evelyn approaches the booth.

She has a smile that means "I don't know what this nerdy stuff is, but I'm glad you're having fun." I have seen that same smile many times. "Hey, keep going, don't mind me," Evelyn says, holding back a laugh.

I glance at the ship to estimate how much time I have until I need to guide the next person in.

"So, you stuck here with Chester the whole night?" Evelyn says, making a face like she just ate something spoiled, holding the expression until she chuckles.

"He's not that bad," I say.

Evelyn gives the smirk she saves for when she doesn't believe you.

I put my hands up in surrender. "Fine. You're right. But I'll be done in a few. I'll catch up to you."

"I heard the baking club made French toast doughnuts. Better figure something out before they're all gone," Evelyn says, shrugging as she walks away.

I continue advertising the booth, all the while searching for any other members of the sci-fi club. After a few minutes, I see Ben. *Perfect.*

"Ben!" I call him over.

He approaches with a look of skepticism. "Hey, what's up?" Ben is a full foot taller than me. So even though he's great to talk to, especially about his fan theories, it always ends with a cramp in my neck.

"I'm gonna need you to take over for two hours. I have to step out."

"I don't even have a uniform," Ben whispers. Whenever he argues, Ben does the opposite of what most people do. He gets quieter and quieter.

"I have extras!" I pull out the bag of uniforms and remove the largest one. "How about, if you do this, you pick the next movie we watch at movie night?"

"I dunno. Why do you have to go?"

"I said I'd hang with Evelyn at the festival and I…I was gonna…" I press my lips together.

"Make it two," Ben says with a smile.

"What?"

"The next two movies. I wanna pick."

"You're the best! I'll be back in two hours, I promise." I toss Ben the uniform and rush inside the ship. "First Officer Chester, you are now acting captain of the vessel!"

"I'm what?" Chester says, not sure if he's being made fun of.

"You're acting captain, like in the original pilot."

"You're being held on planet Helios-four?"

"Um, sure, something like that." With no further explanation, I grab a small bag where I stashed my normal clothes and race off to the bathroom to change.

With my lucky outfit back in effect, I splash some water on my face and adjust my hair in the mirror. Now, Step four. A feeling of urgency pulls me, like I'm standing on a steep hill, the slope nudging me to move forward. *The bathroom exit is eight feet away. There's also a window to the outside twelve feet away.* No, I'm not done. I force aside the thoughts of escape and check my phone.

## 6:18 p.m., May 4th, one bar of reception, 93% battery.

Okay, in two hours, it's 8:18. "You can do this," I say aloud to myself. "Remember, what's the worst that can happen? She says no?" She could say no! How is that fair? *If she says no, she'll probably never talk to you again.* And without any friends left, I'll be free to work on a time machine to go back before I made the biggest mistake of my life… No, that's not gonna happen. She'll say yes. I can do this. Plus, a time machine is impossible… probably.

I take a deep breath, hoping to breathe in enough courage to walk over to Evelyn, take her by the hand, and ask her right in front of everyone. Unfortunately, the air is distinctly uncourageous. I lower my standard for how much courage I expect out of a deep breath and try again.

Twelve deep breaths later, I settle for just enough bravery to walk out of the bathroom.

I find Evelyn leaning against a wall in the gym with a doughnut in each hand. When she sees me, she tries to wave, nearly dropping one. Somehow she makes being awkward and confident equally cute.

"Hey," I say in a definitely casual best friend sort of way.

"'Sup, what happened to the costume?"

"Not gonna wear that all night, but I gotta be back in a couple hours."

Evelyn nods, offering the doughnut. "I nabbed an extra when they weren't looking. Wasn't gonna let you miss out on this…on three?"

I take the pastry and count to three, then we both take a bite into our French toast doughnuts. Sweet maple accented with a hint of cinnamon and nutmeg fills my senses. It's still hot, but more than that, the flavor itself offers a sense of warmth.

"I will never eat anything this good ever again," Evelyn states.

"Same…we gotta make friends with someone from that club."

"Definitely," Evelyn responds, staring lovingly at her pastry. We finish our food without another word.

"So where to now?" Evelyn asks.

"I heard the Outdoor Activity Club set up a mini-golf thing."

"Lead the way."

As we walk through the gym, the buzzing sound of students laughing and gossiping surrounds us. It all feels like the background, as if we are together in our own tunnel made of noise.

"Wait," says Evelyn. "Let's check this out." She points to a small booth run by the art club. "They put up the artwork from all the best kids in school. I wanna see."

I follow her through the makeshift gallery, and she stops to appreciate every single piece.

"This one is so cute!" Evelyn exclaims, pointing to an oil painting of a bulldog wearing a baseball cap.

"I like this one." I gesture to an abstract painting with jagged lines and bright colors. "You know, you should've joined the art club. You're really good."

"Nah, just a hobby. I'm not that good," Evelyn says.

"Please, last week you drew Ms. Gamallen in class. Way better than anything up here."

"Oh! That reminds me." Evelyn slides her heavy backpack to her front and pulls out a sketchbook. She quickly flips through the pages until she proudly displays a drawing to me.

"Oh, my gosh!" I *literally* jump with excitement. "That's Captain Jacques P. Killian!" She even got the expression just right.

"I knew you'd like it." Evelyn carefully tears it from her sketchbook and hands it to me. "I mostly followed some drawing online. He made that same face in like half of 'em. Only tough part was finding the right shade of red, tamarillo got me pretty close."

"It's perfect."

"Thank you, thank you." Evelyn bows. "But, eh, we have a lot of festivalling to do, so why don't you just put that in your backpack for now?"

The smile Evelyn uses is meant for hiding something. Is she embarrassed about the drawing? It's literally better than all the ones on the wall. "I have a better idea," I say to Evelyn, giving her my most conspiratorial look. After confirming no one is watching, I balance the drawing right on top of another canvas. "See? Right at home."

"Yeah, not bad," says Evelyn, nodding. See? She had nothing to be nervous about.

"Hey! What're you doing!" shouts a member of the art club. The student approaches us.

"Uh-oh!" Evelyn says, grabbing her drawing and my hand. Warmth skates from my hand up to my cheeks. She's holding my hand. She's holding my hand. She's holding my hand. *The plan is working, oh my gosh, it's actually going to work*. Stop thinking about the plan for one second and enjoy this. Did I mention she's **holding my hand?**

Evelyn pulls me through the crowd, running awkwardly as her overweight backpack bounces from side to side. We turn a corner quickly to get out of sight and plop down behind another booth. When we look up at each other, our mischievous grins burst into laughter.

When the moment passes, I pull out my backpack to put the drawing away. While spending another moment to admire it, the corner of my eye catches a frown from Evelyn. Though once I zip up my backpack and stand, her frown dissolves into that same fake smile from earlier. *It's time to move to step five: ask her to the dance.* Not yet though. It has to be at the perfect moment. *You're running out of time.*

"Okay, so, mini golf?" Evelyn says.

"Real quick, what time is it?" I ask.

"Seven fifteen," Evelyn says after checking her phone. "You gotta get back to your thing?"

"No, no not for another sixty-three minutes."

"Precise as always. Sounds like plenty of time to school you in some mini golf."

We take the long route around the booths to avoid being spotted by the art club, and before long we get to a small mini-golf course with four holes. A classmate hands us each a bright neon golf club and a matching ball, green for me, blue for Evelyn.

"You don't stand a chance, Lora Mersha-Moore," Evelyn proclaims.

"Bring it."

"Oh yeah? How 'bout a bet?" she says, stepping closer to me.

"A bet?" I ask, feeling a quick thumping in my chest as she leans in. Almost as if my heart is one of those beach metal detectors, beeping louder the closer Evelyn gets.

"Winner picks what we do next," Evelyn says.

"You're on!"

The next twenty minutes contain some of the worst golfing and silliest trash talk as we make our way through the course. Before long, we have one more left, a classic windmill, and our scores are tied.

I take my shot and get through the windmill but miss the hole in one. I'm close enough that Evelyn needs to make it in one shot to have a chance of winning.

She squares up, preparing to take her shot, when suddenly everything gets quiet, like when the lights go down at a movie. A faint high-pitched noise hums for a moment, like a mosquito ringtone. *What is this?* No one else seems to hear anything, and soon the sound fades away, and only a little dizziness lingers. Then I see Evelyn, standing there like a statue, looking blankly at the wall.

"Hey, you okay?" I ask.

Evelyn doesn't respond.

"Ev?"

She looks up and smiles. "Yeah, just thinking about which booth I wanna check out next." She takes her shot and fails to clear the windmill.

On my turn, I easily secure the win and get a groan from Evelyn, who misses once more.

"All right, L. You win, so where we going?" Evelyn asks as she walks back to the booth. We return the clubs but are allowed to keep the neon-colored golf balls.

"Hmm." I check my phone.

**7:49 p.m., May 4th, two bars of reception, 92% battery.**

Twenty-nine minutes left. Perfect day at the festival, check. *You're not done yet.*

"Follow me," I say, leading Evelyn out of the gym and away from the festival. "You asked me before why I like sci-fi stuff so much."

"Eh, yeah, it's cool, just not my thing."

I take her to a field next to the school and gesture up to the night sky. A canvas of a billion twinkling stars fills each of our fields of vision. A small, blue-tinted comet passes over us, creating a shimmering blue tail. Standing next to her, I take a moment to admire the tapestry of luminescence above us.

"Up there, each of those tiny little dots is a star bigger than the sun, with its own gravity and planets. So many possibilities. Each one of those books I obsess over is someone else guessing what one of those possibilities could be."

"It really is beautiful," Evelyn says, gazing upon the starry night. "Compared to that, I guess we're all small."

I feel my heart bouncing like a slinky on a trampoline. "Evelyn?"

"Yeah?" Evelyn says, still looking at the sky.

I focus on her face, twinkling in the starlight. I made the perfect moment, I did it—*you can still screw it up, then she'll move away and you*— Stop, it's just a few words and—*and everything changes. What if she says no?*

My thoughts are replaced by a fog, like the voice in my head is being choked. I can feel all these emotions pressing themselves against the inside of my chest, wanting to become words. The words I practiced a hundred times. What if they come out as the wrong ones? Or what if they are the wrong feelings?

"Never mind, it can wait," I sigh.

Evelyn remains quiet as I turn away. I can't look her in those beautiful blue eyes right now. Then the scared voice in my head returns.

*Stupid, stupid. How could you think this was a good idea? She doesn't feel the same. She's gonna move away, and the two of you might catch up once every few months. But every other day, you'll be alone.*

"I, um, I guess I gotta get back to the booth," I mumble. *The nearest exit is...nowhere.*

Evelyn still doesn't respond.

Then I turn around to see Evelyn standing in the same spot, looking up. "W-what're you doing?" *Something is wrong.*

She doesn't say anything.

"Are you okay? Ev?" In the distance, Evelyn's blue eyes no longer shine like they usually do.

"What's going on? Ev! Talk to me! Somebody, help!"

Without warning, Evelyn falls limp on the ground, shocking my body into action. I race towards her, but before I finish a single stride, a bright blue spotlight blasts onto the ground from the sky directly above her. From the light, a shockwave knocks me away and onto my backpack. I scramble to my feet and face the bright light. Evelyn's unconscious body floats as if plucked by the stars above. Terror soaks into my bloodstream, forcing me to take a step back. Before I can even get a few inches away, my body stops, refusing to move. *You have to help!* Adrenaline surges inside of me, forcing out any other thoughts. Then I leap into the light.

The moment I cross into the spotlight, I become weightless and start ascending towards the sky.

"What's going on!? Help!" I yell. I twist my head, trying in vain to look around to see if anyone is watching this. Below me, the ground is getting farther away. Above, Evelyn floats thirty feet higher. "Wait! Evelyn!" I try to swim upwards to close the distance.

After minutes of flailing desperately, I am no closer to her. Below me, the field is gone. Instead, I see the whole city. I rise even higher, helpless as the air grows thin. Between shallow breaths, I start to make out a dark shape in the sky blocking the stars like a giant shadow. The blue spotlight pours down from the center of the shadow, pulling us up like an unyielding tide. My lungs protest against the nearly oxygen-less air I give them with small gasps of breath. Then a hole opens up in the shadow right at the spotlight's source. Fluorescent light emanates from the hole, blocking my view of Evelyn.

"Evelyn!" I screech with everything left in my lungs.

As if in response, the hole vanishes in the shadow, and the blue light turns off. Weight returns, and I plummet towards the ground. I fall thirty feet before… **CRASH!**

I plunge through a sheet of glass, and my feet smash against a metal panel with a hundred blinking buttons. I bounce off the metal panel and slam into a chair that partially cushions the fall. My head pulses pain through my skull. Everything blurs, and I smell blood. The massive dark shadow above me shrinks into the sky.

"Ev," I cough.

Unable to move my head, I dart my eyes around to get a sense of where I am. It looks like the cockpit of a ship, almost like the one I built back at the festival. A bright red flashing light fills the room from the dented control panel. A high-pitched buzzing blares all around me, and glass grows to cover the shattered section that I crashed through.

I fade in and out of consciousness. I see the dark shape disappear over the horizon. Then nothing. I see the shape of Earth shrinking in the distance. Then nothing. I see the stars twinkling all around me and a pale blue dot in the distance. Then nothing. I see a giant metallic ring shimmering with red light as the ship I'm in passes through the center.

Then nothing.

# CHAPTER 3

# IT'S ONE SMALL STEP

5/2

Dear Diary, I don't think this whole journal thing is really doing much for me! Prolly another three weeks, and Dr. Davis will have some other thing for me to do? This week was my dad's, and we went to the zoo. I'm supposed to write at least five sentences, but that's all that happened. [4]

~~(does that one count?)~~

Lora's been acting weird this last week. [5]

— Evelyn

♦♦♦

**M**Y SENSES RETURN ONE AT A TIME. First, the smell. It is so sour it almost burns. Then, the feeling of something tugging at my foot, nearly pulling off my shoe. Next, the sound of rain pitter-pattering on stone and the taste of salt and iron. Finally, my vision comes back. I'm lying in a dark, grungy alleyway with city lights shining in the distance. I see a large stone overhang above me, blocking the rain. *Where are you?*

Suddenly, a sharp tug at my foot grabs my attention. Two small fluffy tails peek out from behind my shoe.

"Button? What happened?" I croak. I feel so dizzy I must be seeing double.

An outline of a tiny creature shifts behind my shoe. My head spins like I rode a rollercoaster underwater as my senses fully restore themselves. I blink a few times as my vision unblurs. this is not Button. It's not even a cat at all. The creature has two long white tails, a vertical mouth in the center of its face, and a third eye at the top.

I shriek and shift away. "Ow, ow, ow." A dull pain radiates throughout my body, stopping me from moving nearly as quickly as I want. Fortunately, the sudden movement and noise seems to have scared the cat monster, and it darts away. Where am I? What is going on? *Lying here wondering won't get you anywhere.* Right.

I try to move again, this time expecting the pain. I scan my arms and legs to find countless scrapes and bruises, like I fell into a barrel of cheese graters. Eventually I manage to get upright by steadying myself on a wall made of a strange smooth stone, almost like glass with dark, unmoving smoke trapped inside.

"Ow." I force myself to start moving. The floor has an odd texture, the same clear stone as the wall but filled with tiny holes like some kind of strainer. *Keep moving.* I slowly make my way to the bright glowing lights at the end of the alley.

When I get a view of the sky, I freeze. I must be dreaming. Not one, but two bright full moons illuminate a street. A torrent of sour-smelling rain falls from the cloudless sky, tinted by neon signs with symbols I don't recognize. The alley has an overhang keeping me dry as the water disappears into toothpick-sized holes in the street. Suddenly, the rain stops, and with it, the street in front of me begins to fill. Triangular cars hover off the ground, zipping by. Figures of different shapes and sizes appear from alleys all around, making the once-empty street look lively in a matter of seconds.

Maybe there is a convention going on, but if that were true, I definitely would've heard about—

"Outta the way!" a boy shouts.

Before I can react, a person wearing a dark hood crashes into me at full speed. We both tumble to the ground. Too dazed to do anything, I remain on the floor while the hooded boy stands up.

Immediately, two figures with broad shoulders barrel around the corner and point at the hooded boy and me. "There he goes!" one of them shouts. They each wear a helmet shaped like a clamshell so big it covers their entire head.

The boy scrambles to his feet and runs deeper into the alley. I stand slowly but still have no idea what's going on. One of the clamshell men points their hand, wearing a hefty silver gauntlet, towards the alley. A bright red glow from the gauntlet's palm turns into a blast of light that whizzes past my ear. The light collides with the wall behind me and liquefies a basketball-sized section of the stone.

The heat of the liquified wall washes over me as adrenaline hides my injuries. I just have to run. I roll to my feet as quickly as I can and sprint the only path away from the men shooting lasers, deeper into the alley. "Wait for me!" I call to the hooded boy. He must know what's going on.

The pair of clamshell men chase after me through the alley, shooting more beams of light, melting more walls around me. I catch a glimpse of the boy turning down another path in the alleyway and follow. After turning, I stop at a branch in the path with three directions ahead. And no sign of the boy.

The path straight ahead leads a few hundred feet out of the alley and into the street. The cat-like creature from earlier is strutting deeper into the rightward path, which branches even further. The path to the left has what looks like a dumpster filled with scrap metal and a dead end.

The sound of the men gets closer. Only a few seconds until they will turn and spot me. Assuming they can see through those giant clamshells. Which way should I go? *Think, Lora, think!* I was just behind him. He couldn't have gone forward, or I would've seen him before he got out.

I dart to the leftward path milliseconds before they turn to the same fork in the alley. I rush, as silently as possible, towards the dead end of my chosen path. I duck behind the plastic dumpster and find myself inches away from the hooded boy. A foul smell kicks me in the face, making my eyes water, but I stay quiet.

"Which way did they go?" asks one of the men, still standing at the fork in the alley.

"I don't know. Probably to the right—more places to hide," responds the other.

"Hurry up, let's go!" The two of them run to the right and disappear deeper into the cavernous alleyways.

"Okay, what is going on?" I ask the moment they are out of earshot.

"I was making my escape when you got in the way," the boy responds, still concealing his face.

"Escape from what? Who are those guys? What is this place? Who are you?"

"To your first two questions: the Arbalest. Naibrillar City to your third, and my name is Dwyn. We done here? Good. I'll be on my way."

"Wait!" I whisper-shout, putting my arm against the wall and blocking Dwyn in. "How'd I get here? Is this real?"

"Probably crashed, and yes," Dwyn says as he tries to sneak under my arm.

I try to stop him by sliding my arm down. Instead, I accidentally catch his hood and slide it off.

The sight of his uncovered head freezes me in place. His face is pale purple, almost pink. But not as pink as his eyes that are as vivid as a highlighter. Atop his head, faintly glowing blue lights dance like flames where his hair would be. I stifle a shriek and step back.

"What? Never seen a Lelog before?" Dwyn asks.

"A what?"

"I guess I've never seen anyone who looks like you, either. Where'd you come from?"

"I ... I was at Harthian ... and then I don't remember."

"Harthian? I've never heard of that planet."

"Planet? No, that's my middle schoo—wait, I'm in space? This is space?" My confusion is quickly replaced entirely by excitement.

"Well, no. This is planet Naibrillar. If we were in space, we wouldn't be having this conversation," Dwyn remarks while his pink eyes search for a way to escape.

"You know what I mean. Space, as in, not Earth? I can't believe there's life on other planets. I can't believe *I* found life on other planets," I babble, barely registering what he's saying. Despite his many strange features, his face still looks human. If I ignore the purple-pink skin, give him a wig and some contacts, he could pass as a student at Harthian. Provided the wig was fireproof.

"Well, yeah, there are thousands of planets with life in the Pell Galaxy. You hit your head or something?"

I shake off a layer of excitement, just enough to focus and address Dwyn. "Yes, I am Lora Mersha-Moore, human, from Earth." I give the *Star Voyages* salute. I've practiced that in the mirror a thousand times.

"Never heard of it," Dwyn responds unceremoniously.

"Hmm." Okay, never heard of a human? Maybe there's a different name for us. I rack my brain, thinking of other terms from every book and show I know. "Terran from Sol-3? Does that ring any bells? The Milky Way Galaxy, at least."

"Must've missed that cosmography class. Look, can I go now? I have a, uh, meeting," Dwyn says, his facial expression remaining still.

His mouth movements don't quite match with what he's saying. In fact, it barely moves at all. Dwyn tries to leave again, but in my excitement, I never let go of his hood.

"Oh, sorry." I release my grip, and Dwyn begins walking away, out of the alley. *The plan!*

"Wait! Evelyn!" I shout, memories returning to me all at once.

"E ... Evelyn to you, too?" Dwyn replies, continuing to walk away.

"No. Evelyn is my friend. She was taken. I think. I don't know, but she must be here." I chase after Dwyn. Evelyn has to be somewhere nearby. We were kidnapped at the same time, right? So, she has to be on the same planet. She could be hurt, or worse. An alien monster could be—no, that'll never happen. The monsters almost never get you, unless you are some unnamed guy or have a red shirt on. Evelyn was wearing blue today.

"You should worry about yourself. The Arbalest aren't big fans of off-worlders."

"Yeah, but we have to find her!"

"Plus, I'm not one for daring rescues. Look, I gotta go."

"To your, 'uh, meeting'?" I ask.

"Yes." Dwyn walks away but stops at the end of the alley. "How did you know where I was hiding? I like to think of myself as someone who can at least evade a nosy child."

"Easy. You had to have turned, 'cause it was too far forward for you to be out of sight, and then to the right there was one of those cat things."

"Cat?"

"The little animal thing with the three eyes and freaky mouth, looks kinda like a cat," I explain. "Anyways, it ran away when I made a bit of noise the first time, so if you came charging through, it woulda been heading the opposite way."

"Clever." He pauses for a moment, as if lost in thought. Though his expression remains completely still. "You know what, maybe I do have a rescue in me. If she's been found, she'd be at the Saeth fortress. I'll show you."

I start to jump with excitement, but my scrapes and bruises lobby against it. I get it! It's like the sci-fi books I always read. An adventure to prove myself! Maybe this could actually be fun. I move to follow Dwyn, wincing with each step. "Thank you."

"First," Dwyn starts, "we have to meet with Fais."

Dwyn looks back and forth before gesturing for me to follow. Once we get to the main street, I finally get a full glimpse of the alien city. Creatures with the same clamshell-like helmets fill the street, though most are much smaller than the two that chased us before. Buildings with unrecognizable symbols in neon colors drown out the light from the twin moons.

"Who's Fais?" I ask.

"Someone I owe a lotta money to."

"So just like a quick trade, then off to find Evelyn?"

"Well... I don't have it."

# CHAPTER 4

# GAZING AT CLOUDS

**D**WYN PULLS ME THROUGH THE STREETS, weaving through crowds without so much as glancing at another alien. I don't know how he does it, because I can't get enough of the bizarre inhabitants of Naibrillar. Neon signs with complicated symbols paint the ground in a warm glow. I try to memorize each of the symbols, but no obvious pattern emerges.

A creature resembling a lion made of vines with two wings shaped like the leaves of a banana tree walks past me on two legs. So majestic! As another alien passes, a shiver runs down my spine. Four curved blade-like legs skitter towards me, held together by a human torso with a spider's head wearing a strange hat. *Please don't eat me, please don't eat me, please don't eat me.* The creature stops right in front of me for a moment before continuing on.

"What was that?" I whisper, still trembling.

"Him? He's from Corryn. I think he likes you," Dwyn says.

"Corryn? Got it, note to self, never go to Corryn." Though a little shaken, I don't let that stop me from soaking in every detail. After I find Evelyn, we will have to explore— *Don't forget about the plan. The dance, the perfect summer. We're already behind!*

I shake my head to refocus. "So, who is this Fais person, really?"

"I told you; I owe her a lot of money."

"Yeah, but why?"

Dwyn's face remains expressionless. "We made a deal. I was supposed to rob the Saeth fortress, then Fais and I split the profits."

"And?"

"Well, you saw those guys chasing me. Plan didn't go right."

"So? That's not your fault," I say, stopping in the alien street. "You'll just go back another day."

"Not how it works."

We continue to walk through the street. The lights and sounds are so strange individually, but all together, it's just like any other city. If only it didn't smell so sour, and had fewer spider monsters, this place would be perfect.

"Wait a second," I start. "Are you sure we can just walk out in the open here? You said they don't like off-worlders, and they were literally just chasing you!"

"It's fine. As long as they don't sees us break any rules," Dwyn says, not even bothering to put on his hood.

A sudden realization hits me, something I should have asked sooner. "Wait a second. I have another question."

"Seems like a pattern," Dwyn responds.

"How are we talking right now? I mean, if this is a different galaxy and all, and you've never even heard of Earth."

"Doesn't matter."

"Yes it does! We're speaking the same language; how does that make sense? Is there like a little yellow fish in my ear translating everything you say? Or some kind of telepathy—"

"Nanobots," Dwyn says, cutting me off.

"Nanobots? Wow! That's amazing."

"Yup."

"Um…are you gonna give me any more than that?" I ask.

"You really don't know anything, do you?"

"Not if you keep not telling me anything!"

"Some scientist named Achosi made tiny robots with every known language and spread them around."

"That's so…wait, what do you mean *known* language?"

Suddenly, the sour smell doubles in potency. I cover my nose with my sweater sleeve, and Dwyn looks up towards the sky.

"What's the smell?" I ask.

"Time to go." Dwyn leads me away from the center of the street.

"What's going on?"

"Rain."

Rain? Why does that matter? Either way, I hurry after my new companion. Better to follow someone who knows this world. Eventually we arrive at a canopy overhanging part of a sidewalk. Aliens of all shapes and sizes press together underneath. In an instant, the street is completely clear. Earlier I enjoyed observing all the unique alien life, but this is way too close. I can count six different species that I'm squeezing between.

Then the rain starts. It looks like any other rain, but barely any clouds are in the sky. All the huddled creatures press themselves against the buildings as if to get as far away as possible. The droplets collide unceremoniously with the glassy stone ground before disappearing down the toothpick-sized holes and becoming lost in the smoky shapes in the rock. Maybe these aliens are allergic to water or something?

A crowd like this shouldn't bother me. I've been in tighter packs at sci-fi conventions, but at least they were all the same species! My breathing becomes shallower and faster. This is the first moment since arriving that I've really had the chance to stop and think. *You are in another galaxy.* Don't freak out. *How could you not freak out, you are so far away from home that*—I try not to finish the thought. I can't even imagine the distance. *It's more than the distance traveled by every car, plane and boat in human history combined.*

I clench my hands together to stop from trembling, but it barely helps. *The nearest exit is straight ahead...* I'm packed so tightly that I don't even feel like I'm outside anymore. I have to get away, I don't care if I get a little wet in the rain, I have to move.

I squeeze myself through the crowd and towards the empty street. Dwyn reaches out and snatches my arm. "What're you doing?"

But it's too late. A light mist hits me and my whole body begins to burn, like I jumped into the shower on the hottest setting. I screech and leap back, tumbling to the ground.

"Can't you see! It's raining," Dwyn shouts.

I frantically rub my face with my sleeves to get off as much liquid as I can. My lucky sweater quickly starts to discolor. I suddenly realize it isn't hot. It burned me, but it isn't hot.

"That isn't rain! What the heck was that?" I squeal. The pain has mostly stopped, except for the small cuts I woke up with. Those still singe like when my dad put medicine on scrapes back home. Though this rain is probably not good for my wounds.

"It's called sting rain," Dwyn explains. "Avoid getting caught in it next time."

"Noted." I wait for him to help me up, but when he doesn't offer for a few seconds, I get up on my own. *Don't be so stupid, Lora! You watched every episode of* Star Voyages. *You should at least know better than to jump into acid.*

Minutes pass before the acidic rain dies down. The whole time I can feel the aliens judging me for doing something so dumb. But eventually, they leave the huddled canopies and return to the street.

"Ready?" Dwyn asks.

"Let's just go."

Soon, Dwyn ducks into an alleyway, and I follow. "These alleys are a maze, just like before when the guards chased us," I say. "Why is that?"

"Don't know," Dwyn says as we press deeper into the alleys.

"Maybe like some kind of irrigation for the rain? Or, or service tunnels for some kinda futuristic power grid?"

"Doesn't matter."

"What about—"

"We're here," Dwyn interrupts. "All you have to do is stand there and be quiet, okay?"

I nod. Wait, am I meeting a space criminal? Am I a space criminal? No, those Arbalest people are obviously the bad guys, so that makes us the good guys.

Dwyn checks to make sure no one is watching before knocking twice on a door made of hard plastic. The door swings open, letting out the smell of batteries. Through a short hallway, we enter a dimly lit workshop.

Scraps of metal and wires litter the room. The only piece of furniture is a metal table covered in tools I've never seen before. Floating in the center of the room is a single cloud.

Out of the fog of the cloud pops a black sphere the size of a base-ball. It doesn't fall to the ground but instead points towards Dwyn, then to me. My skin prickles. *Space Voyage aliens were not this creepy.*

A voice comes from the cloud. "How unexpected. I thought you might have fled the city." The cloud's voice sounds like a quiet thunder with a distinctly feminine quality. Clouds can talk here? How does it speak? How does it eat? Does it eat? If it has to pee, is it just like raining? *Focus, Lora.*

I look towards Dwyn, wanting to let out a barrage of questions, but I hold my tongue. It's not my turn to talk.

"Well…" Dwyn starts. "Fais, it didn't go as planned."

"Oh?" The cloud starts to turn slightly gray.

Dwyn pulls out a small gadget shaped kind of like a calculator with wires sticking into it. "I tried, after a second it locked me out. The guards were on me. I had to run."

"Is that meant to get you out of our agreement?"

This cloud is gonna kill us. Dwyn doesn't look scared, so I shouldn't be either. But… Dwyn's expression never changes. *The exit is eight feet away.* Could I even escape? Where would I go?

"Come on, Fais!" Dwyn appeals.

A bolt of lightning jumps out of the cloud towards the table, and a few of the gadgets light up for just a few seconds. This display causes the flame on Dwyn's head to die down to half its size. Surprisingly, this makes me less afraid, more angry. I want to yell out "Don't let her talk to you like that, Dwyn!" but I force myself to stay quiet.

"Look, I'll go back and get it all. And she's gonna help me." Dwyn gestures towards me. He thinks I can help? Like I'm some kind of secret weapon? Of course I am, like a hero from a story who saves the day and makes it home before the dance.

"I was wondering about the girl. Regardless of who you bring here and what claims you make, the truth is you were meant to arrive with the money, and you haven't. Perhaps you took it all for yourself." Fais darkens to a deep gray, and electricity sparks from the center of her cloud.

"Wait!" I jump in front of Dwyn. I don't care if it's my turn to talk or not! The black orb floating in the cloud snaps to point towards me. "I saw Dwyn getting chased by those guys, the Arbalest. He is telling the truth."

The room falls silent, and Fais changes back to her original white color. I can't believe I'm arguing with a cloud.

"Plus," I continue, "Dwyn is a good person. He saved me from that rain, and he said he's gonna help me find Evelyn!" Right as I finish speaking, the pain from my cuts and bruises flare, causing me to wince and tremble.

"What a peculiar child, Dwyn." Quiet rumbles sound inside the cloud for a brief moment. "I will allow you two days."

"Got it," Dwyn replies.

"All right!" I go to give Dwyn a high-five, but the fast movement shocks my injuries again. I retract my hand with a small yelp.

"Hey, Fais," Dwyn starts. "Do you have any Elicyf for her?"

"Elicyf?" I ask.

"For your cuts. They seem minor enough."

"They don't feel minor!"

"Of course. You will find it in the back room," Fais replies. A few tiny sparks appear on the side of the cloud, and a key floats off the desk and levitates next to her.

Dwyn walks over and snatches the key from midair. "Carbon or silicon?" he asks, looking at me.

"What?"

"You. Carbon or silicon?"

"I… What?"

Dwyn sighs. "You said you are a human, right? Are they carbon-based or silicon-based? It is a different medicine depen—"

"Um, carbon," I say.

Dwyn nods and leaves through the back door. Then I shake my head. "Wait! There's silicon-based life too?"

Dwyn walks out before he is able to respond, leaving me alone in the room with Fais. *The exit is nine feet away.*

"You are wrong," Fais says in a low voice, like thunder from miles away.

"About what?"

"He absolutely would lie and keep it all for himself, just like his father."

"His father?"

"He's all that boy ever talks about," Fais says. The thunder sounds in distinct pops, almost like laughter. "If he hasn't mentioned him, you must have just met. Why would you stand up for someone you just met?"

If this dumb cloud read half the books I have, she'd know. The first step in situations like this is to happen upon a wise guide. The guide is always trustworthy!

"I just know, okay."

"Peculiar."

Dwyn returns from the back with a small vial of black liquid. "Got it," he says.

"Time for you to vacate my workshop." After she lets out a few small sparks, a couple of components float off the table towards Fais. They snap together midair as though held by invisible hands. "I have much to do. Do not forget what you owe me."

How does she pick stuff up? Is it like an electromagnet or something? *Stop getting distracted! You have a mission.*

"Two days," Dwyn says as he hurries out the way we came in. I follow, and before long we are back in the alley leading to the crowded street.

"So, that was Fais," I say.

"Yup."

"Nice of her to give us that medicine."

"That wasn't—" Dwyn starts. "It doesn't matter."

The blue fire on Dwyn's head changes slightly. It is still the same color, but the way it flickers is somehow different. "What's going on?" I ask.

"Fais and I made a deal: She gave me a device to open the gate, in return she gets 1,200 Taithirs' worth of stuff after the job—about a third of my expected take."

"Okay."

"Well… Device didn't work. Now, if we don't get her the money plus extra for that medicine, she'll kill us."

"That's not fair!" I shout, and the sudden outburst flares the pain in my injuries again. I lean against a wall for better support.

"It is fair. She's doing what's best for her, we're doing what's best for us."

"If you can't pay and she…you know." I gulp. "Wouldn't that mean she never gets her money though? Seems like a bad boss."

"She's no one's boss. She sells what she builds and needs her customers to be scared enough to pay up. Letting us go is another chance to get paid. Killing us raises the odds no one backs out in the future. She did the math and made a choice, just like anyone else would. The medicine was part of that," Dwyn explains. "To her, we're all just Glyfs who scurry off, and sometimes come back with money, other times we don't."

"Glyfs?"

"Pests from Lelog, they'd sneak into homes and steal food. Not important. No one does anything just to be nice. Don't trust anyone."

"Fine, we get the money, and we save Evelyn all in one swoop." The plan doesn't change. It's just a branch off the main plan. Step 4.1: break into Saeth. Step 4.2: find Evelyn. Step 4.3: find a way to get home. Then that branch merges back into the main plan. *The dance!* Now that it all fits into a neat sequence, I let myself get just a little excited. I stood up to a literal cloud monster! She could shoot lightning. And now, I'm going on an infiltration mission to a space compound filled with evil guards. They'll have lasers and crazy tech! The sci-fi club is going to love this! *You can't tell them until you get home, which means you have to concentrate!* "Let's go."

We walk through the street. With each block, it becomes less and less crowded until it is nearly empty. The bright neon lights are replaced by tall, lifeless buildings. After a few more turns, Dwyn stops.

"We're here." He gestures to a thirty-foot-high circular fence that surrounds the area of a small neighborhood. Imposing gray structures form a perimeter past the fence. Dwyn remains standing a few hundred feet away from the edge as more men with clamshell helmets patrol the area.

No, those aren't helmets, are they? Why did clamshell heads evolve on this planet? Maybe it has to do with the rain? *Think about that later. Evelyn could be just behind that fence.*

"So Evelyn is gonna be in one of those buildings?" I ask, scanning the area.

"Probably," Dwyn answers.

"What's that mountain in the middle?" I point to a lumpy hill, taller than any building I've seen on this planet.

"The Arbalest doesn't let people bring anything from off-world. Anything they find, they toss in the pile."

"Everything?"

"Yup."

"Clothes? Or what if a kid just has a toy or something?" I ask, but Dwyn doesn't respond. There's so much. How many people must've had their stuff taken to make something that big? And what's that at the top?

"Let's go," Dwyn says.

"That ship!" I point towards the apex of the hill. At the very top, a small ship is jammed, front-first, into the broken metal. The spaceship looks like a plane the size of a small truck. It has a dome-shaped glass roof, two wings, and thrusters in the back.

"Shh," Dwyn says as a few of the closest guards look towards us. Dwyn quickly puts on his hood and pulls me aside. "We don't want to draw attention."

"That ship at the top," I continue in a hushed tone. "That's how I got here. I fell through that glass. It's the last thing I remember."

"Then how'd you end up a few blocks away?" Dwyn asks.

"I don't know, but the ship can get you, me, and Evelyn out. Now how're we getting in?"

Does that mean the person who took us is in there? If it's anything like the books, the alien abductors are there waiting for a big confrontation.

"There's some planning to do, but once we get in, we just have to sneak over that hill to the other side," Dwyn explains.

"Over that? One of these guards is definitely gonna see us!"

"Not if we're quiet. Plus, they're pretty easily distracted."

"What about going around? Wouldn't that be safer?" I ask.

"Going over is the fastest way to where they take the off-world prisoners, so if you want to save your friend, that's the way we go."

"Okay, but I was just saying—" I start, but Dwyn gestures for me to be quiet.

He leads me to a nearby alley and continues. "Anyway, we'll figure it out in the morning."

"Wait, we're not going now? But the people who took me might be on the ship, and what about Evelyn? She could be in there!"

"Quiet down. You'll be no use to her if we get caught. There are only three gates to get in, and they are all locked by passcode or keycard." Dwyn's tone is sharp and final.

I can't object to making good plans. "Fine, we do it tomorrow," I say. "We gonna form a team?" That's what they do in heist movies, at least.

"Always do a mission with the smallest team possible," Dwyn says as though he's practiced the phrase. An alien crew pulling off a daring heist would be cool, but whatever saves Evelyn the fastest is most important. *The dance is in two weeks.*

"So, Dwyn," I say, as I follow him through the zig-zagging alleyways. "I've been thinking. That ship is what got me here. But it only took…" In a flash, I realize in all the commotion I never checked my phone. How long has it even been? I quickly reach into my pocket and pull out my phone.

## 1:21 a.m., May 5th, No Service, 88% battery.

Light years away in just a few hours? That means we can get back the way we came in no time at all.

"What is it?" Dwyn asks.

"I remember the ship. Then some sort of… You know the show *Astrogate*? It looked kinda like those."

"The what?"

"Guess you don't get the science fiction channel here. Okay, it was shaped like a big metal doughnut."

"What's that?"

"You don't have doughnuts here? No wonder you're so grumpy. Anyways, it was like a huge silvery circle." Oh, my gosh, I haven't eaten since the festival.

"A quantum tunnel?"

"Ooh, quantum tunnel, I like the sound of that. Yeah, could that've gotten me here?"

"Tunnels are linked and let you cross any distance instantly, so likely that's—" Dwyn starts.

"Like teleportation? So faster than light travel is real? How does it work?" I start bouncing up and down.

"If I knew how a quantum tunnel worked, I probably wouldn't be spending my evenings hiding behind dumpsters and dealing with people like Fais."

"Fair point." My stomach growls after being reminded of my last meal.

"Do you have any food? Please tell me aliens eat food."

"We'll eat in the morning. You'll just have to make do until then." Dwyn stops at a dead end with the sound of rushing water flowing nearby.

"Hey, what's that noise?" I ask.

"Just past this building is the only freshwater river on this hemisphere. This building used to be a treatment plant to take some of the sting rain out."

Dwyn presses his hand against a small plate attached to the smooth stone wall. The sound of beeping chirps from behind, and the wall slides open.

"Whoa! Is that a handprint scanner or a hidden switch?"

"Y'know, you don't have to ask every question you think of. Is that a human thing?" Dwyn walks through the hidden doorway.

I stick my tongue out at Dwyn before following him inside. Behind the doorway is a massive warehouse filled with broken-down machinery and stacked dusty plastic boxes. Other than a small metal track that slides the door open, every surface of the hideout is stone or plastic. "This is where we rest for the night."

"You have a secret hideout!" I've never been in a secret hideout before. Unless the sci-fi club counts. Most students don't know where it is, so it's kind of like a secret.

"Uh, I guess," Dwyn says.

"That's so cool!"

"Whatever. Sit down, show me your cuts."

I sit against a strong plastic box and roll up my sleeves to show my arms. He takes one of them roughly.

"Watch it!"

This close, Dwyn doesn't look as human as I thought at first. Tiny purple-pink scales cover his face, each shaped like a hexagon, so small that I couldn't see them until now. His eyes are slightly too far apart, and his pupils are the wrong size. The more I look, the less human he appears. Dwyn takes the vial of black liquid and drops some on each cut, one by one. I brace myself, preparing for a sting, but instead it feels like warm Jell-o.

"So Dwyn."

"What?"

"You're a good person, right?" *That's a stupid question. No one can answer that for real.*

"Sure," Dwyn replies. The blue flame on Dwyn's head starts to move so quickly, it almost looks like it's popping.

"It's just... Fais mentioned your dad."

Dwyn pauses before continuing to apply the medicine to my cuts. "What about him?"

"Nothing, just mentioned him, is all." *Drop it, drop it, drop it.*

Dwyn sits back, all of my wounds properly Jell-o-ed. Dwyn's fire slows down and twists in spirals while he remains silent.

"I'm sorry, never mind," I falter.

"He's trapped in there. Same as your friend. I'm trying to get him back."

I knew it! "We'll get them both back. Step one: find a way in. Step two: find Evelyn and your dad. They're probably in the same area."

"Well—" Dwyn interjects. Can't he tell I'm planning?

"Step three: get what Fais needs. Step four: sneak to the ship and fly to safety. Step five: figure out how to get home. Step six—"

"This is a waste of time." Now, Dwyn's interjection stops me.

"Wait, what? Weren't we supposed to be planning?"

"You don't even know how we're getting in. Planning that many steps ahead, when anything can go wrong earlier, is pointless."

I open my mouth to respond, but what is there to say? That doesn't make any sense. Problems like this need plans, it's as simple as that.

"Every one of those steps could go wrong," Dwyn continues. "Then everything afterward falls apart. A good plan is clear in the short term and flexible in the long term," he says like it's another practiced phrase.

I can tell it's my turn to respond now, but there is no reasoning with someone who doesn't value a good multi-step plan. He's probably just worried about his dad. I should say something; I can't have my teammate nervous on mission day.

"Don't worry, we'll save your dad tomorrow."

"Sure. Anyway, the cuts should heal up in an hour or two."

"Great! Thank you, Dwyn."

"We'll go over plans in the mornin—"

"Wait!" I interrupt. "How do you even know what an hour is? Aren't those based on the sun and Earth?"

"There you go with the questions again." Dwyn turns his back on me and walks towards a corner.

"Aren't you curious about everything out there?"

"All I want to know is when I can be done babysitting you," Dwyn says.

"Babysitting? How old do you think I am? How old are you?"

"I'm fifteen years old."

"You're barely older than me!"

"So?"

"Wait! How do you know what a year is?"

"Can we just get to sleep?" Dwyn responds and walks away to

one side of the room. He picks up a yellow orb, about the size of a watermelon, and drops it onto the ground. As it falls, it unravels, transforming into a large, hammock-like cloth that hovers just above the ground. Dwyn steps onto the floating fabric and lies down.

"Is there another one of those for me?"

Dwyn does not respond.

"I'd happily take a non-futurey-floating mattress instead if that's easier!"

Still no response.

I storm to the opposite corner of the warehouse and lean against the wall right under a window. The moment I do, all of my exhaustion hits me at once. So I get as comfortable as I can, using my sweater as an improvised pillow.

In the silence of the alien night, thoughts of the unimaginable distance between me and home return. Dread seeps from my head down to my heart. Evelyn, Fais, Naibrillar, home. It is all too much to think about, so I take that dread and stack it neatly on the top of my "deal with later" pile, leaving just one thing on my mind.

Step four: have the perfect night with Evelyn at the festival. Step five: ask her to the dance at the most perfect moment. Step six: have the best summer ever before Evelyn has to move.

# CHAPTER 5

# HOPE AND FEAR

~~5/5~~ 5/6

Dear Diary, if someone finds this journal, my name is Evelyn Stewart, I was kidnapped from Harthian Middle School, Opinville on May 4th. I think I've been in this place for 2 days. I can't tell. I wish I could hear someone's voice, even a Gamallen lecture would be like a symphony. I'm so bored, I guess this journal is good for something, right Dr. Davis?! Also, why couldn't I have been kidnapped by someone with good food, anything instead of these gross carmine-red crackers, how is that fair!

-Evelyn

♦♦♦

My stomach groans, interrupting my fragile sleep. *Get up; it's a school day.* No, yesterday was Saturday, remember the festi— I shoot up, immediately awake. Dull boxes stacked haphazardly and an overwhelming sour smell prove that I am still here. Barely any light passes through the window above me, so I take out my phone. There is no way a text is getting through from Earth, but I check anyways.

## 11:38 a.m., May 5th, No Service, 57% battery.

Mom and Dad must be so worried. Did they call the police yet? *You will be in so much trouble when you get home.* Noticing the battery, I quickly return the phone to my pocket. As I sit up, my injuries don't hurt at all. That Elicyf stuff really did the trick.

"Finally." Dwyn starts descending the stack of boxes. "Humans sleep so long." He tosses me a bright red wafer. "Breakfast. Hurry up so we can get to work."

Finally! I grab the wafer eagerly and stuff half of it into my mouth. The taste is vile, like burnt rubber and baking soda. I gag, but my stomach is so empty I can't even throw up. *If you don't eat, you'll die, and you won't be able to save Evelyn.* Fine, I continue eating but look for a way to distract myself from the awful taste. "Hey, Dwyn?" I say.

He looks up but doesn't respond.

"Why are all the buildings here made of this weird smooth rock?"

"It's quartz," he says, as though that explains everything.

"But why is it so dark and smoky looking?" I ask.

"I don't know, that's just how it looks."

What kind of guide doesn't know anything? Whatever, it's time to get planning. I swallow the last bit of alien food; soon, I'll be back home and will never have to eat something so bad again.

"Anyways, how are we pulling this off?" I think that's how a pro would say it. Definitely.

"I've broken in three times before," Dwyn says.

"Then what's the plan?" I hop to my feet. "Some kind of tele-porter? Or a jetpack!"

"Slow down," he cautions.

If he got in three times, why didn't he save his dad then? *Stop worrying; we need to stay on track!*

"First," he continues, "they used to just have one passcode." Dwyn sits on a plastic box. The blue flame on his head illuminates his pale lavender face as the only source of light in the room. "Only had to figure out the code once, but then they started changing it every few hours."

"So we figure out a code and use it before they change it?" I know this situation is severe and dangerous, but finally being able to stop and make a plan feels so good.

"Well… we don't know when they change," he says as he starts digging through one of the boxes. "The second time, I had to be patient. They had security drills every seventeen days. The computer would simulate an error. The keypad would show negative one, and the gate would unlock."

"So the keypads are all connected to the central computer? And if the computer goes down, the gates are open?" I clarify.

"Yup, but now it's at random times, so can't use that anymore."

"Okay, how'd you get in the third time then?"

"With this." Dwyn pulls out a small device from the satchel. "Fais made this for me. That's why she wants her cut."

Oh! So he had to make a deal with Fais just to save his dad. That makes sense.

"You connect it to the keypad, and it'll try every combination of five digits in a second."

"Really? That worked? That's…" I look down while I do some quick arithmetic. "A hundred thousand combinations. Fifty thousand tries on average before it gets it right? I can't believe they would allow that many attempts," I say, proud of my mental math.

"Well, I guess I showed them their mistake." Dwyn carelessly tosses the device back into the bag. "Now it stops accepting passcodes after five failures. With three gates around the perimeter, we could make fifteen guesses—"

"0.015% chance," I interject.

"Sure, whatever. Point is, not a good plan anymore. I tried that yesterday, and you saw how that turned out."

I start pacing, trying to think. "So what is your idea, then? Figure out the code with some kinda pattern?"

"No, my new plan is much simpler," Dwyn says. "All we have to do is steal a keycard from one of the guards."

"That's it?" I say, feeling disappointed. "That seems way simpler, and I thought we'd use some sort of cool alien tech! Plus, why didn't you do that before?"

"You saw those guards; if they caught me pickpocketing them, with those gauntlets of theirs..."

A shiver runs down my back. "Fair enough, but what do you need me to do?"

"Simple. You distract, I pickpocket."

My jaw drops. "Um, me? Distract? But they could... Won't I...? Isn't that dangerous? How would I even distract them, anyways?"

"Well... think of it this way. Maybe they know the answers to your questions. Plus, if things go wrong, you can always run away."

"That's not very comforting. Are you sure there's not some sort of gadget? Like a translocator beam or something?"

"A what?"

"Never mind." *For Evelyn.* Right, I have to do this. I stand up and put on the most confident voice I can. "Let's go." I can't believe my last meal is gonna be that gross red thing.

After a rather embarrassing time using a bathroom not at all designed for human anatomy, Dwyn and I set off through the winding alleyways of Naibrillar. It's so dark despite it being daylight. This planet's sun is dim enough that I can look right at it without squinting. The dual moons are no longer shining in the sky, and the neon lights are all off, making daytime even darker and more dreary. "Keep an eye out for a solitary guard," Dwyn says.

We press up against a smoky quartz wall underneath a small overhang, waiting for a guard. *You have to move; Evelyn is in danger, and it's your fault.* No, it's not, what did I—*You brought her outside in the open.* How was I supposed to—*What if they were after you and got both of you instead?* Could that be? I am the one always thinking about space and aliens. What if that made me a target somehow? *The nearest exit is...* I look around. There are plenty of ways out if I need to run. Unlike before, I'm not surrounded by any other aliens... not even Dwyn. What? Where is he? How long have I been alone here? My knees feel limp as I push myself away from the wall. Then a drop of liquid falls on my hand.

Just one droplet makes my hand feel like the worst sunburn of my life. I retract my arm as another droplet hits my shoe. I don't feel that one, but the fabric of the shoe starts to dissolve. I wipe my hand dry and rub my foot on the ground until it stops dissolving.

A deep stomping sound carries over the soft droplets of acidic rain, and an Arbalest guard walks around a corner, acid bouncing off of his clamshell head. *All your exits are gone. There is no way out.* I try not to move, to become invisible, but there is nothing to hide behind. He stands up tall and faces me, sting rain droplets still running down his clamshell head, though he seems not to mind.

"State your name, off-worlder!" the guard shouts. The clamshell doesn't move; instead, the words echo like there is a speaker inside the shell.

"Um, I'm—" I stumble backward as the guard raises the tremendous gauntlet. *Think, Lora. Think, say something, anything.*

"I am Captain…um… Lily Pelerne! I was sent here by the Federation." I try to put on my sci-fi-club-president voice.

"What … who?" the guard responds.

"I am here to run an inspection of the Arbalest compound. Your superiors have all the proper paperwork."

"I didn't hear about any inspection," the guard says.

"You didn't know?" Keep stalling, just enough to wait out this rain. "I'll have to put that in my report! Can't say I'm surprised though. They only send me to planets when things get really bad."

"Ambyra sent you here? But you sound like a kid!"

Just then, I spot Dwyn gesturing for me to keep going from behind the guard. He came back? *Of course he came back, you're his secret weapon, remember!*

"Me? A kid? With how disorganized you are, you'd think your whole operation was run by kids. I heard you had multiple security breaches!"

He lowers his gauntlet, and a quiver appears in his voice. "We tightened up security since then," the guard tries to explain. "And I wasn't even working those days, so it's not my fault!"

Dwyn reaches into the guard's pocket carefully and pulls out a small badge the size of a credit card with strange symbols on it. Nice going. Even the rain looks like it's about to die down. This might actually work!

"Now, go fetch your supervisor and have him report here immediately!" I command.

The guard begins to turn around when Dwyn makes a panicked gesture. What now? I look at his hands and see the card is attached to the guard's uniform by a thin wire from his chest.

"Wait!" I shout, dropping my sci-fi-club-president voice for a moment. Dwyn, with one hand on the wire and one hand on the card, tries to separate them with force.

"What is it?" the guard responds. How has this guy not noticed yet? I gotta learn how to move that quietly. *No time to learn, you're going home soon, remember.*

"Where are your manners? You are speaking to a captain. No salute, no respect for the rank! Wait until—" What was her name? Oh, right! "Wait until Ambyra hears about this!"

"Oh, I'm sorry, ma'am," the guard says, bowing his head and fumbling over his words. He quickly stands upright and gives a salute, putting his fist on top of his head.

"What is your name, officer? I think the folks at command will wanna hear about you."

Dwyn carefully pulls out a small device with a red switch. He flicks the switch, and a reddish-orange blade made of light appears, creating a dim glow on the floor behind the guard. Whoa! They have laser blades! I'm gonna have to get me one of those.

"I am Laz," the guard responds, holding his salute. "Is that all, captain?"

With a quick swipe, Dwyn slices the wire and slinks away.

"Yes, Laz, go find your superior and let them know I have arrived." I try to repeat the salute back.

Laz begins to hustle towards the compound. Right before I can bolt away, he turns back. "Wait a second," the guard begins. "Can you show me proof that you are a captain?"

"Proof? What do you mean proof?" Dang it. We were so close!

"Anything to show me you are who you say you are." The guard begins raising his gauntlet again.

"You mean like a badge?" I ask.

"Sure."

"Well, how do I know you work for the Arbalest? Where's your badge?" A smirk creeps up on my face.

"It's right here." The guard reaches into his pocket and finds it

empty. He feels his chest for the wire and follows it to its end, smoldering and badgeless.

While he stands dumbfounded, I barrel away at top speed. Even at my fastest, the guard starts to gain on me easily. I spend a lot more time binging TV shows than I do exercising. But with enough quick turns, I might be able to lose him, even if I can't outrun him.

Before long, my legs refuse to run any farther, and I stay as still as possible against a wall. Relief builds in me over the next few minutes with no sign of Laz. I start to walk slowly back to the hideout.

Why are these alleys such a maze? I can't find anything in here. There are so many paths, and they all look the same. At least I'm moving; I can focus on that. After many wrong turns, the sound of flowing water tells me I'm close to the hideout. Soon, I find Dwyn leaning against a wall, twirling the wire with the card at the end of it. Everything that just happened finally hits me, and I burst out laughing.

"You gotta teach me how to be so stealthy," I say. "He didn't have a clue."

"Sure, maybe. You weren't so bad yourself," Dwyn says. The blue flame atop his head burns just a little bigger.

"Thanks. You could say I was … yanking his chain." Of course, I laugh at my own joke.

"What?"

"It's a joke! What, now you're gonna tell me you don't have jokes in space?"

"We do. Just good ones."

"Hey! Come on, that one's funny. If you were from Earth, you'd love it."

"I doubt that," Dwyn starts. The shade of blue fire turns cool, and it shrinks back to a normal size. With it, he speaks in a more serious tone. "We need to focus on the next step. We need a plan for once we're inside. Let's get back to the warehouse."

"Yeah, to the hideout!" I say, and I begin to lead the way. Dwyn steps forward to walk ahead of me. He spins the card around in small circles by the severed wire as we approach the hideout. I swing open the door, and we step inside. Finally, something going right. I'll be back home with Evelyn in no time. And then we can get right back to the plan.

**ZAP!** A beam of bright red light collides with the metallic track on the sliding door above us. I dive to the ground, narrowly avoiding the molten metal. Across the room stand two Arbalest guards, their ridged clamshell faces protruding towards us. The warmth from the molten metal hits me like an open oven, and one of the guards aims, his gauntlet glowing brightly. Before the laser fires, I try to roll away and stand. The laser collides with the floor, and a tiny droplet of the superheated metal splashes up my shoulder. I shriek as my sleeve ignites into flame. I swat at the fire frantically, putting it out before it can spread.

*The nearest exit is...blocked.* The door we came in is partially melted, making escape impossible. There has to be another way. *The exit is... one hundred feet away.* Across the building is a single window that overlooks the river. Dwyn is already rushing towards it, and I do the same. One guard goes after him while the other fixates on me.

"This one matches the description of the keycard thief," the guard says into a small device on his wrist. I take cover behind a small pile of metal boxes. I should've known they had communicators. They do in every movie!

"Surrender now or face the consequences!" the guard yells as his gauntlet begins to hum.

I grab a surprisingly heavy plastic box and do my best to lob it at him. His gauntlet fires, liquifying the box midair. The liquified plastic flies towards the guard, who sidesteps to the center of the room. I charge towards the window, staying close to the wall to keep as much distance as possible from this clam monster man.

On the other side, Dwyn struggles to hold on to the badge as the other guard tries to yank it from him. I get to the window first, narrowly avoiding all of the guard's attacks. I swing the window open; it leads to a fifty-foot drop into a massive river below. The strong wind pelts my nostrils with a sour sting.

Both guards are now focusing on Dwyn. The first is still gripping the keycard, and the second smacks Dwyn's arm with his gauntleted hand. Dwyn stumbles backward, losing his grip. A red mist streams out of his arm like a can of spray paint. His blood is a gas? That's so— *You have to help!* I feel my thoughts fade away, I leave the window and charge towards the scuffle.

"Don't hurt him!"

Dwyn deftly dashes away for a chance to reach inside his satchel. He pulls out his glowing red knife made from light. With a single swing of the knife, the guard is forced to drop the keycard. I dive onto it and grab the keycard with both hands. The wind is shoved out of my lungs as my chest slams against the stone floor.

Dwyn swings his knife again, causing the guards to step back, and he takes this chance to sprint to the window and dive out before the guards catch up.

While the guards are momentarily distracted by Dwyn, I roll to my feet and rush to the window, still gripping the keycard.

On the windowsill, I freeze. *It's too high, you can't.* I try to step forward, but my legs shake as if trying to liberate themselves from my instructions to move. *You can't jump, you're just a scared little girl who couldn't even ask Evelyn one stupid question!* No, that's not true, I can do this. I try to push myself forward, but the harsh taste of the air forces me away. I turn back, but a giant clamshell blocks me. The guard grabs at the keycard, trying to rip it out of my hands. I pull back with all my might, and when I lose my grip, I tumble backward down the fifty-foot drop.

# CHAPTER 6
# BEACH

**Wind whips around me,** and a sharp sour smell cuts my nostrils as I plummet to the river.

**SPLASH!** In the blink of an eye, I am deep underwater. My eyes burn, and my mostly healed scrapes singe once again as I claw towards the surface.

Even with my head above water, I can't open my eyes; the pain is too much to bear. I flail my arms to try to find some sense of where I am. The pungent water's current moves back and forth, splashing into my nose and spinning me around. I gag, which allows more water into my mouth. Dwyn told me this river was freshwater, but the years of sting rain mixing with it makes it as sour as lemon juice, without any of the flavor. Like the river is made of vinegar. Luckily I manage to find a massive pillar, presumably holding up the structures above. I hug the pillar as tight as I plan to hug Button when I see her again. She won't enjoy it, but I need that hug.

I get my head well above the surface and breathe hard through my nose to force as much water out as I can. I cough and cough until eventually I catch my breath. I wipe furiously around my left eye until it is dry enough that I can squint and see out of it. A hundred feet in one direction is a beach. *This is gonna suck.*

I take a few deep breaths and release my grip on the small reprieve the pillar provided, falling back into the water. I swim towards the shore as best I can, which isn't very well even in normal water. With each stop to take a breath, a little of the warm, vinegary water flows into my mouth. I nearly throw up a dozen times on the way.

After what feels like an hour, the touch of rocks on the shore is more comforting than my bed after a long day at school. I heave myself forward, getting out of the horrid water and collapsing on the beach. I cough over and over, keeping my eyes shut tightly.

Minutes of lying on the beach later, the pain subsides. Slowly, I work up the confidence to open my eyes. Dwyn is sitting right next to me. "How long," I cough, "have you been there?"

"Just after you fell. You lost the keycard?"

"We can get a new one," I say after taking several breaths. Each word I say feels like it scratches my lungs.

"They are on alert now that they've seen us. I doubt they'll fall for it again," Dwyn says.

I lie on the powdery sand, saying nothing. I never want to move again. *You messed it all up!* Just stop, let me breathe. *There goes the plan, and now you'll never get home and never find Evelyn.* Please, I'll find a way to fix it, just stop.

Dwyn continues, "And now they've found the warehouse, so we don't have anywhere to plan, and all my stuff is gone. This is all I could save." Dwyn takes out a small bag and dumps its contents onto the sand. Inside is the knife, the disgusting crackers he tried to pass as food earlier, Fais' passcode-breaking device, a pair of binoculars, a few silver cubes, and the yellow sphere that turns into a mattress.

I sit up, determined to find a solution. "What are those?" I ask, pointing to the cubes.

"They release a bunch of smoke."

"Could we use that? To get in, I mean?"

"They'd see the smoke," Dwyn says.

"We could use the binoculars to watch someone put in the code and then rush up and—"

"Then we'd have to go right after someone else. If they turn around, we're dead, and if we wait too long, they could change the code," Dwyn retorts. "Plus Fais only gave us two days. She won't let it go again."

"Okay. What if we use her device to input the code?" I pull off my acid-soaked sweater and start to wring it out. So much for it being lucky. "Can we get it to work from far away?"

"Don't think so, and even if we did, how would that help?" Dwyn replies, not even taking time to consider the idea.

"I don't know! I'm just trying to figure it out. Maybe your hammock bed thing could bounce us over the fence somehow? No, it's way too high. What about you? Got any ideas?"

"We just have to get out of the city and hope Fais doesn't find us."

"But what about Evelyn? And your dad!" I leap up.

"Only option left." The blue light above his head moves in a slow swirling rhythm. I can't quite explain it, but it's like it dances to a sad song.

"What if … what if we make the error happen?" I say, as an idea comes to me.

Dwyn looks up. "How are we supposed to do that?"

"The device you have, can we make it send a negative number?"

"I don't think it can. Why?"

"Earlier, you said the keypad shows a negative one when there's an error, and when there's an error, the door opens, right?" I ask.

"I guess," responds Dwyn.

"So maybe it's set up to open if the keypad says a negative number!"

"Well… doesn't matter. All the numbers on the keypad are positive, same with the device," Dwyn says, losing interest in my plan. There's gotta be some way to do it. We don't have weeks to watch a dumb gate.

"Wait!" I exclaim, the idea forming fully in my head. "The passcode, how long was it, five digits?"

Dwyn barely looks up. "Yeah?"

"Okay, what if we give it a six or seven-digit number? Can your device do that?"

"Uh, I guess, but the codes are five, so it'll be a waste."

"I'm not trying to get the right code," I say, feeling a smile creep onto my face.

"I don't understand," Dwyn says.

"If it works like computers on Earth—"

"Why would it?" Dwyn interrupts.

"I'm not done! Just listen," I say. "If it works like computers on Earth, then there's a max number it can handle, and if you give it a number bigger than that, it wraps around back to the lowest."

"What? Why? That doesn't make any sense."

"Think of a dial that goes from one to ten. As you turn it higher and higher, it stops when you get to ten," I explain. "But if you found a way to keep turning that dial, it'll wrap around until it's back to one!"

"How does that open the door?" The rhythm of his flame picks up; I can see excitement in it.

"So we know this computer has negative numbers, and when it gets negative one, it opens. So imagine that same dial goes from negative nine to nine. If you try to turn it one past nine, it'll loop around to negative nine, then negative eight, and so on."

"So if you put it nine higher, it'll wrap around all the way to negative one? You think that'll work?" Dwyn asks.

"Exactly! You got it!" I pull my sweater, which is now covered in discolored patches and frayed fabric, over my head. If it has any luck left, now's the time to use it.

"Gimme a sec." I slide away from Dwyn and start doing some math, writing in the sand.

"Now what?" Dwyn asks.

"Figuring out what number we should give it. All I know is it's definitely gotta be bigger than ninety-nine thousand nine hundred ninety-nine since that's the biggest five-digit number. Not sure how much bigger we need it to be." *You don't even know what number system they use.* "We have five tries, right?"

"I thought you were confident about this."

"Um, I mean, it beats waiting around doing nothing. We're gonna have to guess where it loops around, and how exactly the system handles numbers. Don't worry, it'll work."

"Well, we can try it."

"Then we just have to sneak over that hill like you said."

"I've been thinking," Dwyn says. The blue fire on his head twirls slowly for a moment. The movement's flow isn't nearly as clear as before, as if there are layers in the pattern. "Maybe we should try your idea, going around the hill. We might be able to find a path together."

I give Dwyn a smile. "We'll get them both back."

Naibrillar's twin moons rise, filling the dark sky, while the city's neon lights come on one by one, illuminating the cityscape. We approach the compound, still reeking of vinegar but with slightly dryer clothes.

*I'll be there soon, Evelyn, Mom, Dad.*

# CHAPTER 7

# RED KNIFE

5/~

Dear Diary,

Is anyone looking for me? My parents must've noticed by now right? Mom, Dad, if you find me now I promise I'll stop complaining about seeing Dr Davis. See? I'm even writing the journal like I'm supposed to. I promise I'll do whatever you say, just let me come home.

– Evelyn

♦♦♦

**"ARE YOU SURE I CAN'T HAVE THE KNIFE?"** I whisper to Dwyn.

"Positive." He uses the handle of the laser knife to pry behind the number pad. He slides one of the bare wires from the device into a small hole. I gotta make him give me that knife; it's the coolest thing I've ever seen! Dwyn hands me the number device while he continuously scans around, looking for guards.

"Wait, I can't read these numbers, remember?"

"Useless." He takes back the device.

I stick my tongue out at Dwyn. I try to stay calm and playful, like a hero in a story, but my heart thumps so loudly I can feel it in my ears. That just means Evelyn must be close if my heart still works as an Evelyn detector.

With a deep breath, I say my best guess for the number. "Two hundred sixty-two thousand, one hundred forty-three."

Dwyn presses a few buttons on the device, and after a moment, the keypad screen illuminates with strange symbols. *Please work.*

"Wow," he says. "Negative one, you were right." With a loud click, the door swings open, and Dwyn puts on his hood, covering the flame above his head. Close up, there is still a faint glow inside the hood, but the patterns are mostly unreadable. "Only a couple minutes before they'll get here. Hurry."

The massive metal mound in the middle of the fortress casts two shadows in the moonlight as we sneak into the compound. The uneven ground is littered with pieces of strange futuristic machines that look partially dissolved and covered with tiny holes. Why is there so much junk here? What did all these machines do? Why do they leave them out in the sting rain? *Doesn't matter right now, just keep moving.*

I hold in my questions as we hide near a stone building. I check to see if the coast is clear before turning to Dwyn. "Anyways, about that knife…"

"No."

"I got us in. Gimme something to defend myself!"

"Fine. Here." He takes out a pair of binoculars and hands it to me.

"What? I can't fight any space guards with these!" Plus we have those on Earth, so that's no fun.

"Just take them and shut up."

"Excuse me—"

"No. Seriously." Dwyn's tone becomes hushed and urgent, though with his hood blocking most of the blue fire, it's hard to tell what he's thinking behind his blank expression. He quickly crouches behind a nearby pile of broken wires then motherboards and taps his right hand on the back of his left. The gesture isn't familiar, but it can only mean to hide.

After thirty seconds of crouching in silence, two guards jog past us towards the entrance. "We didn't have a drill today, did we?" one guard asks.

The other tilts his head to the side as if stretching his neck.

How did he hear them so much sooner than I did? Maybe his species has special senses. I guess that makes sense. I mean, one of them was a literal cloud. Maybe there could be an alien who—*You almost got caught. Think about this another time.*

The guard stops, and his clamshell head starts to make a quiet clicking noise. "I smell something." Dangit, our clothes! We probably still stink from the river. *The nearest exit is four hundred feet away.* Too far to run. What do I do, what do I—

Dwyn grabs something small and cracked off the ground. It looks like two TV remotes attached together like a boomerang. He lobs the remote as far as he can towards the scrap mountain, and it lands with a loud thunk. The guards leap up, now on alert. They look around, then head towards the noise.

After the guards get far enough away, I turn to congratulate Dwyn with a whisper. "Good thinking with that remote! Now, we need to get to the opposite side of that hill, right?" I point to the mountain of discarded metal in the center. "Which way should we go around?"

Dwyn peeks up from our hiding place and scans the area before crouching down again just before two more guards rush past.

"Left side is out," He says. "Too many that way."

Dwyn starts skulking through the compound, managing to make almost anything into a hiding place. That is so cool! How does he do it? Maybe he could show me. *Don't forget about—* Right, find Evelyn and get home. Then there's no more need for sneaking.

Slowly, we make our way to the right side of the hill, hiding behind a cracked metal orb filled with wires.

"We have an intruder!" a guard's voice echoes from the other side. *You've been spotted. Run!* I fight the urge to flee. If I run I know I'll be seen. Right now I should just stay still, like Dwyn.

"Someone hacked the security system and snuck in," the same voice continues.

"Is it the same thief as before?" another voice asks.

I glance at Dwyn, and we slowly peek out from behind the metal sphere, catching a glimpse of the commotion. Fifty feet away, a dozen clamshell guards stand around a huge man with skin striped like a zebra wearing a large hood over his head.

"Um," I whisper. "What do we do? Maybe we can sneak around—"

"No," Dwyn interrupts, pointing at the Zebra man. "Don't go near that one."

"But he might not see us if we—"

"No, not that way," Dwyn says.

"Why?"

"Won't work."

"So over the mountain?" *You'll definitely be caught and then you'll never find her and never see your family again.* No, it's going to be okay, that was his original plan anyways. He knows what he's doing.

"I…" Dwyn starts. Under his hood, the slight glimmer of blue stops moving for a moment. When it restarts, I can tell it's slower, like a candle about to burn out. Unable to get a full view of the embers beneath the hood, I look to his expression for clues, but still, his pale pink face gives nothing away. "I think that's the only option."

We quickly sneak away from the group of guards until there's a clear path to the mountain. We are so close; I can feel it. "Let's do this," I say as I raise my hand for a high-five. Dwyn simply walks past, ignoring my hand. I guess they don't have high-fives in space. I slap my own hand, as to not leave myself hanging, and continue on.

"You first," Dwyn says.

He wants me to lead the way? He's never done that before. It takes minutes to creep across just ten feet of broken alien devices. Every few steps, to avoid detection, we cower behind piles of shattered technology. I continue to lead towards the mountain of metal fragments in the center of the compound. It stands three hundred feet high, made entirely of scraps and wires. I glance at the ship perched on top, a tiny beacon of black and red color in the ocean of dim gray. *That's the exit. Three hundred feet away…up a hill…made of trash.* With each step, my feet sink and into the piles of old, rusted junk. My legs scrape against jagged edges, not sharp enough to break the skin, but still enough to make sure I won't be comfortable. Each piece looks like it went through a garbage disposal, totally torn up and unrecognizable. Though, even if it were intact, I probably wouldn't recognize the alien tech anyways.

It's hard to believe all this came from other planets, but I don't stop to think about anything besides the task at hand. Each step along this hillside shifts piles of gadgets, changing the terrain beneath my feet. I look back to check on Dwyn only to see he's trailing behind. Why is he so far back? *Something's wrong.* I force myself to calm down. Concentrate on the mission, Evelyn is in a building across this hill. We'll have to figure out how to get home next. Should I ask her to the dance then? Or is it more romantic to say it during this rescue? That's what a hero from a story would do.

As we cross the mountain of metal, large pieces become rare, and my feet sink deep into the loose scrap like I'm walking in the world's pointiest ball pit. *You are exposed, find an escape route.* Right, with nothing big enough to hide behind, a single glance from a guard will get us caught. A storm builds in my chest, but I can't run away either, even if I wanted to. I can barely even walk through this junk pile. I scan the area around the bottom of the hill, and my heart goes from thundering to frozen in an instant. A dozen guards pour out of a nearby building and run in different directions as though they are searching for something. If any of them decide to look up, even for a moment, Dwyn and I will be sitting ducks. There has to be a way, some kind of distraction. I look at Dwyn. He said they are easily distracted, and he's been in here before. He will know what to do. He's even farther back now.

I crouch down on top of what looks like an ancient box TV, big enough to support me. I take a moment to survey my surroundings again. Immediately I see a guard walking up the hill, directly towards me. *Run! Hide! Think of something! Or else—*

**POP!** The sound comes from just beneath me. Below my feet, a glowing red knife cuts clean through the box TV and wedges itself into the hill. I look behind me, where Dwyn hides, his hand extended. He threw it? Why?

"Sorry, Lora. You're the distraction," Dwyn says.

The box TV collapses on itself, and I lose my balance. I fall, dislodging more junk until a small avalanche of broken devices forms to tumble down with me. Finally, I stop rolling and look up only to see a giant clam and a glowing gauntlet pointed directly at my head.

# CHAPTER 8

# ATOWODITE MANEUVER

"**HALT! WHO ARE YOU! WHAT ARE YOU DOING HERE!**" the guard shouts.

I don't respond. I barely even hear him. *This isn't the plan; we were supposed to—*

The guard grabs my shoulder and lifts me like I'm no heavier than a backpack. "You're coming with me!"

I don't argue. The guard's metal gauntlet squeezes around my arm, and any hope I had left is pushed right out of me.

"I found the intruder! Some off-worlder. She matches the description of the keycard thief!" the guard shouts into his wrist communicator. "Captain Rewyth will want to see you," the guard says as he pulls me along.

I look back towards the hill. Dwyn is still there, sneaking quickly while all the nearby guards are staring at me. *He used you as a distraction?* That's... That's... He wouldn't. I can barely keep up while I'm dragged through the compound.

"Hurry up." The guard tightens his grip.

"Ouch! Watch it." The quick stab of pain shocks me out of my quiet stupor.

"Quit complaining, off-worlder!" The guard pulls me onto the central hill to cut across the compound.

I try to free myself from his grip, moving back and forth, but all that gets me is a glimpse of his pale orange skin between his dangerous gauntlets and his uniform. *Think, Lora, think.* There's gotta be a way out of this. Evelyn is so close. The hand on my shoulder looks and feels like metal, but there is an almost invisibly thin clear layer around it. Interesting, but not useful right now.

I struggle to keep my footing as I'm pulled over the uneven ground. "Why do you guys hate people from other planets so much? I never did anything to you!" I shout, trying to buy time to think of a plan.

"You broke into a restricted area, and last night you stole my security card with that rotten thief!" The voice echoes, the clamshell acting almost like an amplifier.

"Oh, when you put it that way… Wait, Laz? Sorry I didn't recognize you," I say. "How do you see with that head of yours? I mean, do you have eyes hidden somewhere?"

"They aren't exactly eyes, but there are tiny holes that let light— wait a second! Did he come here with you?" Laz turns me by the shoulder, putting me face-to-clamshell with him.

"Who?" I ask, pretending to have no idea who he's talking about.

"That thief! He's been stealing from us for over a year!"

"Um…" He's right, Dwyn is just some thief. *Stupid, first person you bump into in this entire galaxy, and you believe everything he says?* What was I supposed to do?

"You did, didn't you!" Laz accuses. "You and the thief must be in cahoots!"

*Dwyn is just over the hill. Just point him out and he'll get caught like you. Get him back!* No, he's my friend, maybe it's a misunderstanding, like when he disappeared before we took the keycard. I just need to talk to him.

"Thief? What thief? No, I came here alone!" I insist. "I was just trying to find a way off this planet and out of your hair—I mean, if you have any hair, which it doesn't look like you do—so if you'd kindly let me be on my way…"

"Not a chance! I'm turning you in, and you'll be sent to the prison compound for the rest of your life!" Laz yanks me along the hill. *The exit is one hundred feet away.* Right! He's pulling me closer to the ship. I just need to slip away for a little. There are no other guards nearby, and—a realization strikes me, interrupting my planning.

"Wait a second, you said I'd be sent to a prison compound? Don't you keep your prisoners here?" I ask.

"What? Prisoners, here? No, of course not. This facility is solely for restricted off-world materials."

"But then why..." I begin to shake in frustration. "He said she'd be..." No, maybe the guard is wrong. *Dwyn lied; he tricked you.* But what about his dad? *Of course that's a lie, and you believed him.*

"Can't you read the signs outside?" Laz asks. "They are posted everywhere."

"Actually, no, I can't. Please, let me go!" I beg. "I just want to go home."

"You're a strange one," Laz interrupts. "What planet are you even from?"

"Earth."

"Earth? Don't know that one. Regardless, the captain will know what to do with you."

Forget about Dwyn, it's just me now. There must be something to do. I have to get to that ship. *He's way stronger, and one shot from his gauntlet and you die.* Right, I can't fight him. Maybe I can reason with him? *He hates off-worlders, and you're from a different galaxy! There's no way that*—wait! An idea hits me like a baseball bat. Episode 10!

"No one's told you about Earth?" I say with my sci-fi-club-president voice. "Well then, my respect for other life forms requires I give you this... warning."

"Quiet!" Laz shouts.

"Earth, um... agents have a substance known as...Atowodite. It's a material and a device that prevents attacks on us."

"Atowodite?" Laz asks. "I've never heard of that."

"Of course you haven't heard of it! It's top secret, used only for defense. Only us high-ranking Earthlings know about it."

"W-what does it do?" Laz falters.

"If any harm comes to me or I press a button, then the device goes off, destroying everything nearby." I reach into my pocket with my free hand and wrap my fingers around my phone. "Completely incinerated! Poof! Just like that."

"That sounds like nonsense!" the guard says as he tightens his grip on my shoulder. I thought it was already as tight as it could get, but now it feels like he could crush me easily. Regardless, I continue my bluff. "I've heard that it's one of the most painful things you can experience. Of course, no one knows for sure because no one has ever survived!"

The guard still doesn't so much as hesitate, so I make my move. *Please work, please work, please work.* I quickly whip out my cell phone, being careful to face the screen away from Laz. "This device might be small, but it sure packs a punch! Just one click of a button, and you'll be done for, so you better release me!" I wait briefly, hoping to let someone else feel a little anxiety for a change.

"You give me no choice." Still holding the screen away from the guard, I use my index finger to quickly turn on the phone's flashlight, an inch away from the clamshell head.

Laz lets out an echoing shriek from within the clamshell. His grip drops so he can bring both of his hands in front of his head. I seize the opportunity and dart away. I'm not quick enough to get far, but with so much junk on the ground I immediately find a place to hide. A large metal sheet covers me completely, and I hold my breath to keep as still as I can. Wow, that actually worked! I knew memorizing all of original *Star Voyages* would pay off.

Laz collects himself and begins shouting into his wrist communicator. "The intruder has gotten away! Mobilize all units. She's still in the compound." He hesitates for a moment. "Also, there is no such thing as Atowodite," he says awkwardly.

I remain hidden and watch Laz head up the hill to get a better vantage point of the compound. Remembering I still have Dwyn's binoculars, I start surveying the area. Guards swarm the perimeter of the compound like angry bees guarding their hive. *The nearest exit is seventy-five feet away.* Except it's up the hill and Laz stands right between me and that ship. If I run, would he be surprised long enough for me to make it? That might be too risky. Everything I've done today is too risky.

I scan the outer pathways of the compound with the binoculars, carefully remaining hidden. In the distance, Dwyn barrels out of a building carrying a satchel. Shortly after, a guard rushes after him, firing lasers from his gauntlet. Dwyn ducks and weaves, narrowly avoiding the deadly beams coming from behind. If there are no prisoners here, why did he want to come? *Don't think about him anymore. Evelyn isn't here. Just get to the exit, seventy-five feet away.*

The commotion grabs Laz's attention from atop the hill. He

charges downward towards Dwyn and his fellow clamshell man. Laz steps on the plate above me as he rushes towards the chase. The heavy boots squish the metal sheet and me into the scrap mountain, but I stay still enough that he doesn't seem to notice, and he continues along to the bottom.

In moments, the two guards surround Dwyn. They're all distracted! Now's my chance. The first guard reaches out and grabs Dwyn, forcing the satchel out of his hands. As it falls to the ground, a dozen small, jagged pink crystals spill out of the bag.

I leap out of my cover and turn to the unguarded ship. A clear seventy-five-foot path to freedom sits in front of me. Before I can even get a few inches towards my escape, my body stops, refusing to move any further. Come on! It's so close. It's not like it's Evelyn down there in trouble, so why can't I move? *You have to help!* Adrenaline surges inside of me, forcing out any other thoughts. Then I turn down the hill.

I place one foot on the metal sheet that hid me moments earlier. With a push from my other foot, the metal becomes a sled, taking me down the steep hill. It shakes like a janky amusement park ride, but in moments, I pick up tremendous speed and slam into the guard holding Dwyn. He is knocked backward, clearly not expecting a teenager to ram into him on a metal sled. I collect my balance and, with all of my thirteen-year-old strength, hurl the binoculars directly at Laz's head, chipping the clamshell and dazing him.

"Didja miss me?" I quip. *Don't just make a joke and let him off the hook like that.* Right, I'll deal with that later.

Dwyn stands dumbfounded. "Why are you...?" Even the fire on his head looks surprised.

I pick up my makeshift sled and turn back towards the mountain. "Run!" The sudden shout seems to get through to Dwyn, and he follows behind. Shortly afterward, a beam of light strikes the ground near my feet. I let Dwyn go ahead while I hold the metal sheet behind us, creating a flimsy shield. Heat conducts through it as the edges get hit. I hold on as long as I can, but three-quarters up the hill, I drop it. *The exit is eighty-one feet away.* I sprint towards the ship with every ounce of strength remaining in me. Beams collide all around, but before any connect, we arrive at the top.

The ship is all black, with red spirals along the sides, and the top is covered by a large glass dome that houses a cockpit, a large

room that takes up most of the ship. Inside, a single leather chair sits in the exact center, and three smaller chairs are evenly distributed around the sides. In front of the smaller chairs, a dashboard filled with buttons, dials, and switches loops around the edge of the cockpit. In the center of the dashboard, there's a massive dent the size of a foot, and the buttons surrounding the dent are cracked.

Dang it, it's empty. If there's no one on the ship, then it probably is the Arbalest's. *They know who took her.* What am I supposed to say? Stop shooting while I interrogate you?

I try to lift the glass to get inside, but it doesn't budge. Dwyn joins in, but still the glass remains. "On three!" I shout.

The guards run up the hill towards us, along with a few more that noticed the chase. I guess they realized their gauntlets are too inaccurate at this range.

"Onetwothree," I say quickly.

Together we manage to lift the glass enough to slip in. We dive into the ship, and I breathe a temporary sigh of relief.

"Now get us out of here," Dwyn says.

"Um, I don't know how to fly this thing."

"What! I thought this is how you got here!"

"It's how I crashed here *accidentally*. Plus, I barely remember it!" I argue. Suddenly a high-pitched electronic sound emanates from the ship. "I guess we just hit buttons?"

"But..." Dwyn starts. Then a laser beam grazes the edge of one of the ship's wings. "On it!" Dwyn says.

The high-pitched electronic sound, now significantly louder, assaults my eardrums. Barely able to ignore it, I hit every button, flip every switch, and pull every lever until something happens. The sound never stops, but eventually a switch gets the ship to hum. Before I hit another button, a laser collides with the ground beneath the ship, and it starts rolling down the hill.

We bounce around as it tumbles. A chair slams into my gut, the ceiling strikes me in my hip, and then I fall back to the dashboard. Out of desperation, I push a lever forward, and suddenly, Dwyn and I lurch back as the ship blasts away from the compound.

I lie on the floor, looking out the window as lasers streak all around, filling the sky like shooting stars.

# CHAPTER 9

# CAN'T DO IT

"**WE'RE IN THE PIPE, FIVE BY FIVE,**" I say as I grip the ship's controls. At least, what I think the controls are. I haven't really figured out what the buttons do yet.

"What?" Dwyn says.

"I heard it in a movie once. I thought it's just what people say." The ship hurls us through the sky above the city, but I tune out the loud noise to think. So I have a ship now, and it's the same ship that took me here. Therefore, it must be able to get me back home. But that doesn't explain where Evelyn is. *You could always try to find a way home without her.* No, don't even think about that. I incinerate that thought and bury its ashes as deep as they can go. I'm not done.

Now, back to planning. Is there another ship here? The planet is more than just the one city; maybe she's on a different continent. Do all planets have continents? No, I don't think they do. Anyways, maybe I could—

"It's not fair!" Dwyn breaks my train of thought. "I had them in my hand! Do you know how much those crystals were worth?"

I sit up and study the fire roaring angrily above Dwyn's head. "Did you really want to break into that place just to steal some crystals?" That can't be it, can it?

"Those were Sydon crystals! They'd sell for thousands," Dwyn shouts. His tone is clearly agitated, but his expression remains unsettlingly constant. "Fais would be off my back with plenty left over to—"

"But what about your dad?" I demand.

Then another frantic, high-pitched noise fills the ship for a moment. The sudden sound startles me, and Dwyn pauses, his hair flame slowly swirling with calm remorse.

"Why'd you come back for me?" he says quietly.

How can I explain that feeling? Before I can find the words, an alarm blares inside the ship, and flashing lights fill the bridge, oscillating between red and violet. I get it, something's wrong, but did they have to fill the ship with the most stressful blinking lights? Then the ship begins to descend. "Why is it falling?" I say.

"I don't know!"

I start flipping every switch on the console, but we only plummet faster. "It's not working!" As we fall, I feel lighter and lighter. I grip the console to stop myself from floating away.

"Try the one from before," Dwyn says.

"I already did!" I slide my forearm across the dashboard, hitting each button. The ship comes closer and closer to the ground. "Brace for impact!"

I hold on as tightly as I can as the ship skids along the ground just outside the city. It bounces, flinging me loose before coming to a halt.

"You still alive?" Dwyn asks, lying on the floor.

"Yup." I sit up, and we both look at each other. Red steam rises from a small cut on Dwyn's neck and twirls with the blue flame before disappearing. I forgot; his blood is some kind of gas. He quickly covers his wound, saying nothing. "Where are we?" I ask.

Dwyn looks out of the glass surrounding the top of the ship. "We must be at least a half mile outside the city."

An expanse of dry plants and dark rocks with random tiny holes like Swiss cheese stretch towards the city aglow with neon lights. "You didn't answer my question," Dwyn starts.

"What question was that?"

"Why'd you come back for me? Why not run to the ship on your own?"

"I wasn't just gonna leave you to be captured!" I try to justify myself, but it doesn't sound right, even to me. I still feel that urge to help, but it's mixed with betrayal and so many other feelings I can't put names to. All these emotions swirl around in my chest, trying to push their way into being words. But I keep them inside. I can't say all that. Instead, I say, "It was just the right thing to do."

"But why?" Dwyn demands.

"Why?" I repeat. "Why are you interrogating me after I just saved you? You're the one who lied to me about everything!"

"Not everything," Dwyn mutters.

"What?"

"Nothing, it doesn't matter. It just doesn't make any sense. You put yourself in danger for me." Dwyn starts lifting the glass dome over the ship. "Everyone is out for themselves. That's just how things work."

"That's no exc—"

"Excuse me," says an electronic voice from inside the ship.

"Who said that?" both of us say in unison.

"Ah, so you can hear me. I've been attempting to communicate with you for the past thirty minutes. I nearly determined you simply lacked the ability to communicate."

"Who are you?" I ask.

"Where are you?" Dwyn asks, eyeing the control panel.

"I am the onboard artificial intelligence for this vessel," the ship responds.

"You're a computer?" I rush towards the console. "That's not, um… offensive, right? You are a computer, aren't you?"

"I suppose you can figure things out, given enough time," responds the ship.

"Did … you just sass me?"

"Why would someone build a sarcastic robot?" Dwyn scoffs.

"Wait, those high-pitched beeps, that was you trying to talk to us?" I ask, completely moving on from my conversation with Dwyn. This is so much better than trying to sort through uncomfortable feelings!

"Precisely. I noticed you two were speaking to each other and figured I would inform you of my status. However, when you dismissed it, I thought it likely that you were simple creatures just mimicking conversation. Fortunately, I was wise enough to attempt speaking slowly so the both of you have more time to process."

"You were speaking so quickly that it just sounded like a high-pitched beeping?" Dwyn asks skeptically.

"You see, I spend most of my time with myself. I often forget how long it takes living creatures to interpret even the simplest data."

The excitement fills my head like a balloon. I can't believe it, a spaceship and an AI! *Remember the mission, that's more*—no, not right now. There is a literal AI spaceship talking to me right now. This is **my** time. I take a deep breath in preparation for my barrage of questions. "Who built you? Where did you come from? Why did you pick me up? Was it the Arbalest? Where's Evelyn?"

"Unfortunately my hard drive was damaged. You can see a rather large dent in the middle of the console."

I … wouldn't know anything about that," I say, vaguely remembering how I fell onto the ship console back on Earth.

The ship continues, "My data storage has been corrupted. I can tell you that I am an automated ship that is meant to belong to a fleet stationed in a much larger vessel."

"How interesting!" I move up to the console, inspecting it from top to bottom.

"Why'd we crash?" Dwyn asks, standing in the back of the ship.

"Simple. I am out of Sydon fuel. Only a small amount was left, and I was attempting to warn you before we took off, but you were so insistent."

"Whatever, I'm done," Dwyn says, lifting the glass to step out of the ship.

"Hey! Where you going?" I say, hopping after him.

"Leaving."

"But wait, don't I get an explanation too? You told me Evelyn was in that place!"

"I said she might be."

"They don't even keep prisoners there. And you have been there before. You knew."

"I told you already, everyone just looks out for themselves. Simple. I do what's best for me, and you'll do what's best for you."

"But what was *I* supposed to do? I can't read the words, and I almost got killed by rain. I'm lost, and Evelyn could be in danger. Don't you care, at least a little bit?"

He turns away, and the blue fire stops for a moment, but he remains silent.

"I wanted to help you, Dwyn, but you gave me this whole lie about your dad just to use me."

"It wasn't all a lie," Dwyn says, still looking away. "My dad, we really did get separated. But he isn't here."

"Where is he?" I ask.

"I don't know. We were on a heist together a few years ago. It went wrong, and he left. He ditched me."

"He can't just leave like that!"

"He had a chance to escape, and he took it," Dwyn replies. His voice doesn't show it, but in the flame on his head there's another layered movement. A pattern that feels remorseful peeks through for just a moment.

"But to go and live somewhere else without even asking you how you feel? That's not fair."

"He did the right thing. He saw a way to save himself."

"No! He was wrong! He should at least have come back for you. Heck, he shouldn't have even left in the first place!"

"You don't know anything about him!" That remorse I saw disappears, and the pattern turns into a display of searing frustration.

"I know it's wrong to just leave someone in trouble!" I retort.

"You don't make any sense! Things were fine before you got here."

"Fine? I remember you being chased by people with laser gloves and owing money to a *cloud*. And again, I came back to save you."

"I used you to get into the compound, and then you try to save me? You ask me questions about every unimportant tiny thing. Instead of worrying about Fais killing us, you're over here befriending some dumb computer!"

"Dumb?" the ship says, interrupting Dwyn. "I'll have you know I can perform more calculations in a second than you can in a thousand lifetimes!"

"I already told you!" I insist, ignoring the ship. "It's the right thing to do. That's all there is to it."

"That's the problem!" Dwyn turns back to the city. "You can't just do stuff without thinking. What if it didn't work? Then we'd just both be caught."

"But it worked! We both got out, so it was the right move." I chase after him. I never thought I would be accused of not thinking something through enough, but in that moment, I really didn't. I can't explain it to him, but I shouldn't have to.

"You took a risk just to save me," Dwyn says. "What's your plan? You must have some sort of reason."

"I don't get why you're so upset. I was the one who helped you."

"Helped me?" A great blue bonfire roars above his head. "My home is gone, the crystals are gone, everything is gone!" Dwyn covers his pink eyes with his hands. "Ever since you got here, everything's different..." Wrinkles form in the hexagonal scales around his forehead as he presses his hands against his eyes. "I've taken more risks in these couple days than the last three months."

Once more, I step towards Dwyn, who's far enough I almost have to yell. "Let's just head into town and get some fuel for the ship. Can't be too hard."

"You want to go back into town? It's crawling with the Arbalest looking for you. You wouldn't last ten minutes," says Dwyn.

"Then I guess we'll have to be sneaky, like before."

"That won't cut it. You don't understand. They know what you look like. You took something from their compound and assaulted multiple guards. You'll be caught."

"Then what're we gonna do?" I ask. "We have to find Evelyn!"

"We? I'm staying as far away from you as possible until this all blows over. And your friend? She's probably dead."

"No! That's not true!" Anger explodes inside of me, launching all of those complicated, messy feelings like shrapnel. "She is alive, and I'm gonna save her! I have to. I'll find her and make it back home and we are going to go to the dance and she's not going to move away."

Dwyn just keeps walking, disappearing over the horizon, but I don't let that stop me. "And I'll do it without you! You'll be hiding from this acid rain while she and I are dancing together a trillion lightyears away! Once I make a plan, that's all I need. Just a plan to fix all of this." I run out of things to shout out into the distance, and I stomp back to the ship. The anger doesn't go away all at once though; it sinks through my body, leaving an emptiness behind that no emotion comes to fill.

The Arbalest had the ship that took us, so they must know where Evelyn is. *You don't have fuel to escape.* Right, first problem, get fuel. *You won't survive on your own.* I can do it. I don't need his dumb pink face.

"So, ship?" I turn to the talking vehicle. "You don't happen to know where I can get some fuel for you?"

"I have not scanned this planet's facilities. However, I estimate there are an uncountably infinite number of ways for you to acquire fuel. I'm sure you'll be able to stumble upon one of them."

*Could've just said you don't know.* "What about the shops in the city? One of them is bound to sell fuel," I say.

"It is likely."

Alright. Step one: find a shop that sells fuel. Step two—*You don't have any money.* Can I trade for it? Do I have to steal it? *How would you even know which store sells it?* Right, I can't read the signs. *Think, Lora, think.* I sit on the ground and run my fingers through my knotted hair. "There is a way out of every box, a solution to every puzzle; it's just a matter of finding it," I recite aloud to myself.

Got it! I understand when people talk. If I hide near a shop, I can listen in and figure out what they sell. *That'll take forever, and you'll be caught.* At least it's an idea. Now, step 2 has to be find Evelyn. I think through everything I've seen, but no ideas come to me. *I just…*

I lie down against the stone, my stomach aching, demanding food. Pain seeps in from the burn on my shoulder from the molten doorframe. I let my arms fall to the ground and shut my eyes, trying to find a solution. It's like four impossible things that have to go perfectly in a row. *I just…*

I'm too distracted to think, that's the problem. I try to take all of this and stack it on top of my "deal with later" pile, but it has grown too high to reach. A droplet of rain collides with the stone next to my head, and the air turns sour. Not now. Please just let me lie here. *I just…*

A few moments go by without another drop, as if answering my silent plea.

"Ow!" I wince as a small bead of sting rain collides with my bare ankle. The rain picks up, and I squirm away. Even getting my body to move a few feet to hide beneath the ship feels just about impossible. With every last bit of effort I have left, I get under the ship, protecting me from the rain. Being inside the bridge would be nicer, but I can't stand right now. *I just…*

Acid rain rolls off the ship around me while I stay dry. Totally drained, I take a moment to position myself where I can see the sky from beneath the ship. I pull the singed, discolored sleeves of my lucky sweater over my hands and look through the thin sting-rain clouds at the night sky filled with stars. With no planning left in me,

I let my mind wander, remembering all the times I showed off to Mom and Dad by naming every constellation from memory. I could even identify a few dozen individual stars by name. However, tonight the stars aren't familiar. I scan the sky back and forth looking for just one single pattern I recognize, until my eyes can't stay open any longer. *I just can't do it.*

## CHAPTER 10
# KILLING TIME

"**Nine pencils, three gel pens, two notebooks,** one sketchbook, a lapis blue golf ball, one journal, my phone, a history textbook, four paperclips, and a hair tie," Evelyn repeats to herself, counting the nicely arranged supplies in the middle of the smooth chrome room.

"Nine pencils." Evelyn reaches into her empty backpack for the thousandth time in hopes of finding something else—another tool, something, anything to help her.

"Three gel pens." Evelyn leans back against her steel bed frame, which takes half the space in this tiny cell. She adjusts one of the pens to make it perfectly parallel to the others.

"Two notebooks." She forces herself to ration the paper when drawing is the only way to fill the time. Tomorrow, she will start on the inner covers.

"One sketchbook." The heavy book's spine is dented from repeated attempts to break down the door. Unfortunately, the sketchbook was nearly full when she ended up here. So it didn't take long to cover every last inch in drawings.

"A lapis blue golf ball." Memories of the festival, of Lora, of home all play in her mind on repeat. Even her mom's new house

that looks like faded wax wouldn't be as cold as the icy white light of her prison. The rest of the room contains only a twin bed, a metal chair, a toilet and a pile of six food trays. At first, Evelyn counted the food trays to guess how long she'd been here, but every time she went to sleep, they disappeared.

"One journal." Evelyn finds the idea of a mostly empty journal alluring. She could fill it with drawings in a day, a whole day she could imagine she was anywhere else but here. However, she promised herself to leave it for her diary. She pictures Doctor Davis' smug look like he's saying, "I told you the diary was a good idea." Part of Evelyn doesn't want to give him the satisfaction. She considers tearing up the journal in defiance. But no, she decided she was going to fill it. That was *her* decision.

"My phone." Dead. With nothing to do, she first turned to playing games on her phone. It died after a day. Now it's nothing more than a paperweight.

"A history textbook." *Vaucela, From the Rainbow War, to the Wizard Myth, to the Modern Age.* Evelyn had complained about carrying textbooks back and forth between her mom's and her dad's, but at least now it gave her something to pass the time. Unfortunately, it is the end of the school year, and History was one of the only classes she did well in. So there isn't much new to read. She liked history, but not so much that she could read a bland textbook more than twice. Though chapter sixteen with the ancient Ylarel poems might deserve a third read.

"Four paperclips." Evelyn checks the door, confirming once again there is no hole for a lock. Evelyn's never picked a lock before, but at least it would be something to *do*.

"And a hair tie…"

Images fill Evelyn's head. The thought of trying to slide notes under the door, some type of trail or clue to where she was. She thinks back to the dozens of times she tried that. She pictures using the pencils and hair tie to make some kind of slingshot or catapult, but no helpful designs come to mind. The only thing left she can imagine is smashing the textbook against the metal walls. The book is heavy, but not *that* heavy. Plus, she already found she could swing the sketchbook harder due to its size.

She slowly unravels a paperclip, being sure not to accidentally break it. She carefully steps over her belongings towards the door.

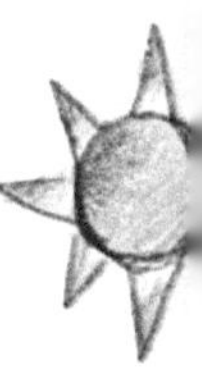

Evelyn slips the paperclip into the thin space between the metal door and the floor and methodically slides it around every crevice it could fit. The door is fully attached on one side, and there's no latch she can find. She moves the paperclip back around, double-checking, then triple-checking, again and again. Frustration builds inside of her until she hits the door with her fist, clutching the paperclip. She screams with all her might, letting all her frustration escape with one exceptional wail. But sure enough, silence returns to the room, just like it always does.

Evelyn's hands tremble as she tries to put the paperclip back to its original shape. With each fold, it becomes more and more delicate until it snaps in two. Evelyn feels her heart snap with it. She knows it can't save her, but now isn't the time to be wasteful.

"Nine pencils, three gel pens, two notebooks, one sketchbook, a lapis blue golf ball, one journal, my phone, three paperclips and a hair tie," Evelyn repeats again, keeping everything carefully arranged in hopes that some solution will jump out at her as she returns to sit near her bed.

A sound captures Evelyn's attention. An electronic beep. Evelyn knows every sound in this place except for this one. Her heart pounds. She knows whatever it is, it can't be good, but at least it is something different. The door slides open. Evelyn hopes to catch a glimpse outside this room for the first time, but instead her view is blocked by a figure with midnight blue skin. Evelyn jumps back fearfully, with just enough care to avoid disturbing her organized supplies.

The stranger's skin changes from its dark blue to crocodile green. "Hello, Evelyn, is it? My name is Arwein. It is a pleasure to meet you." Arwein's skin slowly changes back to its original hue.

"I... What... Where am I?" Evelyn stutters, her voice hoarse like she has forgotten how to speak after all this time.

"You're a long way from home. This is the Pell Galaxy, many light-years away from Earth, I'm afraid," Arwein says. The sympathy feels rehearsed, like when Doctor Davis says he understands how she feels.

"No, that's not... aliens aren't..." Evelyn starts shaking, and her eyes dart away from the creature. She pictures what this strange figure would look like if it weren't for the inhuman features. She tries to explain it all away as tricks of the light. Arwein can't be an alien; there is no such thing.

After a deep breath, Evelyn looks back up and quietly watches as

Arwein's skin transitions along the same gradient, passing through navy before stopping at the same midnight blue. Evelyn's body turns cold and sweat drips from her forehead. "I want to go home. Why am I here?" Evelyn whimpers.

"Don't worry, Evelyn. I'm here to help you, but you will have to trust me." Arwein gracefully moves to sit at the one chair, leaving the doorway. On its own, the door slides almost all of the way closed, leaving just a small gap with the wall.

"Let me out of here! Please," Evelyn begs.

"I would love to. However, I have to know we're on the same side." Arwein's voice remains warm without a hint of hesitation, as though every sentence is scripted.

Evelyn plays a scene in her head. She imagines getting up, sprinting towards the door, and sliding through that gap, all before this strange alien reacts. She plays it over and over again as if teaching her muscles what to do.

"Okay, so… How did I get here?" Evelyn asks, still shaking but starting to collect herself.

"That is a good question," Arwein starts. "I came upon you just a short time ago. I can't say how you came to this galaxy, but after I found you, I hoped we could become allies, so I brought you here and made sure you were fed and rested."

"W-what? Allies? What are you t-talking about?" she stammers. No matter how many times Evelyn repeats the escape in her mind, she can't get her heart to beat slower, her brow to stop sweating, or her hands to stop shaking.

"I want to help you, Evelyn, but that is only fair if we help each other. Wouldn't you agree?"

"I…You'll have to tell me what you want from me," Evelyn says, trying to hide her suspicions. She clasps her hands together to stop them from shaking.

"All in good time. How about the food I've been providing? Human taste buds are quite different from those found in this galaxy. It has been a challenge to find anything you would deem edible," Arwein explains, as though Evelyn should be thankful.

"Eh, it was tough to get down at first," Evelyn says.

"You've been drawing, right?" Arwein gestures to one of the notebooks. "May I?"

Evelyn stares at Arwein's outstretched hand. The sight of the

blue and green skin feels fake. Six humanlike fingers gently reach towards her sketchbook. Her heart thumps louder and louder as the evidence of her being in space becomes overwhelming. She forces her mind to cut out any thoughts other than the visualization of her escape. With enough repetitions she can even feel how her body will squeeze through the gap.

"Okay, sure." Evelyn nods.

The six-fingered alien picks up the notebook with visible respect. "This is most impressive." Arwein flips through the pages, displaying a soft, sympathetic smile. "You have a talent."

"Thank you," Evelyn replies. She knows she has to run, but after being so starved for interaction, she'd happily share a conversation with anyone—even if that person is a creepy alien with blue and green skin.

Arwein leans over and gently returns the notebook exactly as it was. Evelyn sees this as her chance. Just as she practiced in her mind, she leaps up and sprints into the small gap in the door. She sucks in her stomach and forces her way through, all before Arwein can even stand up.

The smell of hospitals and burnt steak fills her senses as she exits her room for the first time. There is a new sound, like a dull humming. Just outside her door is a metal room the size of a basketball stadium, with thick cables running along the ceiling. Towering directly in front of her is a giant man with cracked slate skin.

With a quick movement, so fast Evelyn can hardly react, the man grabs her with a single hand. Evelyn punches, kicks, and bites to try to get free, but the man's skin is as hard as stone. Her knuckles bleed, her toes bruise, and her teeth throb without so much as a flinch from the stone man. He pulls her towards the room but pauses to allow an unfazed Arwein to step out of the fully open door. "Meet my good friend Fydlon. He thought you might try to run, but I was holding out hope."

"Just let me go!" Evelyn shouts.

"How disappointing." Arwein frowns. "It seems you don't trust me. How can I help you if you don't trust me?"

"I…" She hesitates, all hopes of escape leaking out of her.

"It was a mistake for you to rush out like that, but that's okay. I forgive you." Arwein taps Evelyn's shoulder. "Perhaps we'll try again in another few weeks." Arwein smiles warmly and walks off.

"No!" Evelyn screams. "I'm sorry!"

The giant stone man, Fydlon, tosses Evelyn back into the room like a ragdoll, and the door slides closed.

"Wait!" Evelyn rushes back to the locked door "Please! Come back, I won't run, I promise!" She pounds on the door with her fist, tears running down her cheeks. "I trust you! You need my help, right? Just come back! I'm sorry!"

Evelyn sinks to the floor and lies at the foot of the door, hoping to hear footsteps, anything to hint what's happening outside her prison. After a long silence, the tears covering Evelyn's face dry, and she slowly stands up and limps towards her bed. She puts no effort into avoiding her carefully laid out supplies. She steps on her nine pencils, snapping many of them in half.

# CHAPTER 11

# ENTIRELY ON MY OWN

WHEN I OPEN MY EYES, familiar posters of sci-fi heroes welcome me on my mint-green walls. The sound of Button's paws pitter-patter across my desk. My sheets keep me warm as a gentle sunlight pours through my window. Any second, I'll smell breakfast wafting from downstairs. I inhale deeply, looking for a sweet maple scent. Sour. Why is it so sour?

Right, I'm not at home. Instead of a soft mattress, stone presses against my back. Instead of safe walls, I'm surrounded by a cold metal spaceship dripping with acidic rain droplets. Instead of posters, I am greeted only by my bleak reflection in the chrome beneath the ship. *Get up.* My gray eyes look almost lifeless. My hair, which I dyed so carefully a week ago, now looks like a tangle of scraggly copper wires. My "lucky" sweater is nothing but a discolored, wrinkled mess. Is my mom waking up now? Did she think I was there in my bed, even for a moment? *Get up.*

Sensation leaks out of me, until my body becomes numb. The stone isn't pressing on me anymore, the air isn't sour, nearly every feeling flows away. All that's left is a tiny tug, like an invisible string tied around my heart that tries to pull me forward. I wish it would stop and let me just stay here, but it keeps pulling. Or if it won't stop, why can't it pull harder? Then I could just let it guide me along. Instead, it's just enough that I can't ignore it but have to do this all on my own.

My eyes flick back to their reflection. "Get. Up," I hiss through my teeth. With that, I crawl out from under the ship and stand. I can do this.

The city glows in the distance in front of me, appearing much larger now than it did last night. Before I even take my first step, my body freezes, not letting me move at all. *You don't have a plan yet.* I have the start of one. I can do this.

"I'm gonna go find some fuel." I try again to walk towards the lights, but I still freeze. "First," I say to the ship, "let me hide you a bit." I walk to a group of nearby bushes, foraging for some large branches to conceal the ship.

"It is unlikely that you will be able to provide sufficient cover," the ship explains. "There is less than a point one percent chance that any of those twigs will prevent me from being seen."

"It's better than nothing," I retort. Each collection of bushes is surrounded by dry bark that appears to be ripped apart. Almost like it's been burned, but there are no scorch marks. The living plants, however, are covered by a thin, dark green sap. *Eat it.* I don't have time to worry about food right now, so I just ignore it.

"Instead of committing to such ineffective behavior, you should follow the course of action most likely to find fuel," The ship beeps. "There is no reason to delay."

"It's not that simple!"

"Yes, it is," the ship explains. "The city is directly east from here. It is a straight path."

I slowly place the branches on top of the ship. When I finish, my empty hands start to shake. I can do this, follow the plan—*the one with four impossible things.* I should get more branches. I head farther from the city to find more scraps to cover the ship. In the distance, the ship continues to fuss, but I tune it out.

My stomach wails again, and I am hit with a wave of weakness. *Eat or you die.* Right, I can't save Evelyn if I'm this weak and hungry. That must be why I can't get closer to the city. I find one of the still-living bushes and carefully pluck off some leaves. The thin film around them starts to foam at my touch. This is gonna suck, isn't it?

*Please don't be poison.* I shove a handful of the leaves into my mouth and try to chew as fast as I can. I thought it would be sour, but instead it tastes like broccoli-flavored soap. My stomach isn't fully satisfied, but it's not begging for any more gross foamy plants, so I continue gathering branches.

Eventually, my hands are full again, and I return. As I do, the pestering from the computer becomes too loud to ignore. "I will never understand why biological life forms are so insistent on wasting time."

"I'll never understand why someone made a computer that's such a baby!" I say.

"I fail to see the comparison. My computational power far exceeds that of any living child," the ship responds as I cover it sparsely with leaves and branches.

My hands shake again, and I stop as I look towards the glowing lights in the distance. *Every minute you waste is another minute Evelyn could be captured or hurt.* I can do this. I'm not done.

"Then that'll give you something to think about while I'm trying to get us out of here." I walk towards the city without waiting to hear the ship's comeback.

I slink through the labyrinth of alleys, avoiding the heavy boot sounds of Arbalest guards. The sting rain from last night fills the city with the smell of chrome and acid. At the edge of an alley, I find a small poster with my picture on it. It is covered in symbols I can't understand, but the image makes it seem like a wanted poster. Wait, how did they get that picture? I tear it off the wall and stuff it in my pocket. It'll be over soon; it has to be. Then Evelyn and I will be at the dance, and we can all laugh about the time I had an alien wanted poster.

Across from the alley, there is a line of storefronts. I look both ways, waiting for a momentary gap in patrolling guards, and quickly dart across the street to another alley.

After a few overheard conversations without mention of fuel, I feel it's time to move on. I tiptoe deeper into the vast network of alleys throughout the city. After searching for several minutes, I find another collection of storefronts across the street. Once again, I wait for an opportunity and run across.

"Stop!" a voice shouts.

*No, no, no. Can you not screw up a plan just once?* Two Arbalest guards point their palms at me. *The exit is fifty feet away.* I dash through the sea of strange aliens towards an alley fifty feet through the street. The sound of stomping tells me the two guards are just behind me. I duck and weave through the crowd, but that slows me down even more than them.

"Stop now, or we'll shoot!" a guard yells.

I can almost feel the warmth of the gauntlet on my back, but I make it to the alley, and I pivot inside. A bright flash of light stops me from moving any farther. Stone turned liquid pours from a wall, creating a shallow molten pool right in front of me. It's too wide to jump. Maybe I can lose them in a building? No, they might have me trapped if there's only one entrance. What if—

My train of thought crashes as a metal hand slams me against the nearest un-melted wall. I fall to my knees and try to squirm away, but it's no use. I barely manage to turn around. Inches away from my face, a giant clamshell, four times the size of my head, covers my field of vision. Gauntlets hum around me, and all other noises in the street fades. Calm down, just think. The Arbalest had the ship in the first place, right? So they must know where Evelyn is.

"Take me to your leader." I put my hands up in surrender. A guard grabs my right shoulder roughly and hoists me up. With the gauntlet on my shoulder, if he chooses to fire I'd lose an arm in an instant. Any thoughts of resisting dissolve away in my head.

The other guard pulls out a device, which looks like two metal buckets attached by a thick wire. He shoves my hands into the buckets and the metal shrinks until tight. Attached like this, my hands are cuffed and completely unusable behind my back.

Onlooking aliens of a dozen species watch me as I'm hauled through the street. "Any chance you let me leave? I just want to go home!" I plead, but the guards don't respond.

A massive rectangular structure made entirely of darkened quartz towers above every other building in the area. An occasional glass window with metal bars inside is the only interruption on the smooth, smoky surface. I'm dragged to the wide front door locked

with a keypad just like the one at Saeth.

When he types in the code, maybe I can get away. I glance on either side to see guards staring at me, or at least what I assume is staring. Maybe not.

One guard steps forward to the keypad. He raises his arm to type in a code, and then he freezes. He turns towards me, as if he is glaring, though the clamshell never changes. He raises his other hand and covers the keypad as he types in the code.

Inside, I pass through an office made of carefully arranged cubicles. Guards in full uniform sit, barely fitting in each cubicle like an adult at a child's desk. Each stops their work to stare in silence as I pass. What did I do that was so bad?

"Where are you taking me?" I say, but I receive no answer.

Farther in, I'm pulled to an elevator. I try to twist my body gently, not enough to seem like a threat, but enough to see how strong their grips still are. Still too tight to even have a chance. The elevator door opens, and I'm pushed inside.

"Hey, watch it!" I protest.

The guards pile into the elevator, ignoring my outcry. After a few seconds, the elevator stops at the top floor. I'm pulled along another thin hallway. On the left, I pass a series of glass windows protected by metal bars. From this high, I get a clear view of the vinegar river flowing in the distance, cutting through factories and warehouses.

At the end of the hallway, I am taken through double doors to a massive room. A man with zebra-striped skin sits behind a metal desk the size of a dining table. He wears a navy uniform, and a dark hood hides the top of his head.

That's the guy from the compound! He doesn't have a clamshell head, and I thought they hate off-worlders. Or maybe there just is more variety in the species? *Don't get distracted. This is your chance to find out about Evelyn!*

Behind him stand two more guards, one with a pitch-black clamshell and one completely pale. The room is surrounded by windows, still barred, overlooking the city from every direction. On the desk are stacks of papers, each about half as tall as me. The zebra man moves his attention from the abundance of papers and strikes me with his gaze.

"So you're the one everyone's been talking about," the zebra man says with a deep, resonant voice.

"I mean, maybe?" I say, looking around.

"You've been on Naibrillar just over two days, and already you broke into one of our fortresses, stole one of my men's keycards, impersonated an officer, assaulted multiple others, and cost us thousands in damages," the man says.

"Um, well, I read somewhere that a society that gets rid of all its troublemakers goes downhill," I reply. The zebra man doesn't respond immediately, so I add, "Um, who are you, exactly?"

"I am captain Rewyth of the Arbalest, protector of Naibrillar!" booms the zebra man. His tone is confident and powerful, but his expression remains completely unreadable.

"Oh, well, Captain, nice to meet you." I clear my throat and try to put on my sci-fi-club-president voice. "I have come to visit you in peace and with goodwill," I say. "My name is Lora Mersha-Moore. Maybe you can help me. My friend was—"

"Help you? Why would I do that? You are a danger to the people of Naibrillar. You are to be held here indefinitely."

"Me? A danger?" My official voice drops almost entirely. "Do you think I'm some sort of criminal mastermind? I'm just trying to go home!"

"You'll have a new home, a cozy little holding cell ten floors belowground."

"Wait, wait! That ship, the one from Saeth, did—"

"The one you stole?" the captain interrupts.

"Um, yeah. But it's your ship, right? Why did you guys kidnap me and Evelyn? And where—"

"Kidnap? My ship? What are you talking about?" The captain leans back in his seat. "Ah, I see. I was warned you would try some kind of trick. That's your ship. It crashed into Saeth the same day you started committing your crimes."

*It's not theirs? Someone else took her?* That can't be right, but Laz did say they only keep off-world stuff there. Guards from all around step towards me. "Wait! Before you take me, please, have you seen any other humans, anywhere? You know, like me? She would've come here on the same day."

"So, you have an accomplice. You thieves are like Glyfs. If you find one in your home, more must be scurrying close by."

"Please, just listen!"

"I won't be tricked so easily, girl. My brother was a thief, just like you. I even worked with him for a time, decades ago, but this—" He gestures to the large office and soldiers all around him. "This is greater than anything he could steal. I know how you thieves think. You will not fool me."

"No, I told you!" I approach the captain. "I'm trying to go home, but my best friend, Evelyn. She was taken too."

Gauntlets hum all around me, but I keep walking forward. "I don't know how I ended up here, but she must be somewhere close by!"

Rewyth pauses momentarily, still showing no expression. "No one has entered our planet's atmosphere in the past six days other than you," the captain says coldly. "Regardless, you are to be held for your crimes. Take her away!"

I stop in the middle of the room and drop my cuffed hands. *She's not here. She's not here. She's not here.* The guards grab me by the shoulders, but I am totally numb to their coated metal grips. I try to burst forward but am unable to move. "Wait, no! That can't be right," I protest. "She has to be here. She's got to be somewhere. I ... I have to find her, just make sure she's okay."

"Take her to holding cell STT-05," the captain commands.

Evelyn has to be here. It's the only thing that makes sense! That's how the stories always go. I run through dozens of adventures I've read and hundreds of episodes I've watched to figure out what to do next, but nothing fits. I thought I was in some kind of story, with a clean and neat ending. But as that foundation crumbles, I start to feel like I'm falling. *The exit is…the exit is…* It doesn't matter; it's over. I feel every thought in my head float away, every plan, every story that doesn't fit. I don't even remember how to breathe.

Then the strong yank of a gauntlet on my shoulder snaps me back to the moment. *You have to help!* It doesn't matter if something fits. Evelyn is in real danger, and I am not done.

"Wait!" I yell, resisting the guards' pull as much as I can. "You said you monitored the ship coming in. Did you at least see where it came from?"

"Why does that matter?" the captain asks.

"I have no idea how I got here. One day I was on my home planet, Earth—"

"Did you say Earth?" Rewyth says. His voice conveys a hint of intrigue, but still, his striped face barely moves.

"Wait, you've heard of it?" I nearly jump with enough excitement to hit my head on the ceiling, but the guards stop me from gaining any height.

"It's irrelevant now. Take her away," Rewyth commands. The guards start to pull me out of the office.

**BOOM!** The sound of a deafening explosion fills the room. The windows shatter, and dense smoke pours in. Glass shards go flying, and the guards holding me lift their hands to cover parts of their clamshell heads. The taste of metal hits my tongue, and I can't see anything through the thick smoke. I start to move away when a clearly non-metal hand grabs my wrist, just above the shackles.

"Are you okay?" a familiar voice asks.

"Dwyn?" I whisper.

"Let's go."

# CHAPTER 12

# THE MOMENT I KNEW

**"I CAN'T SEE ANYTHING,"** I whisper under the sound of Arbalest guards coughing. Or a sound that I assume is clamshell coughing but is more like the noise a spray can makes. The smoke stings my eyes like I stared at the sun for too long, so I squeeze them closed. The smell of fireworks wafts through the captain's office.

Dwyn pulls at my arm, firmly guiding me through the uneven ground of crushed glass and broken metal. My still-shackled hands make my movements unbalanced, but with Dwyn's help, we manage to leave the office and come to a stop.

"You have to jump," Dwyn says.

"Jump? Where?" I ask, my eyes shut to avoid the smoke.

"Two steps ahead of you, the window is open. I'll get you to the edge, but you'll have to jump."

"Out the window?" I say, stepping back. *It's too high, you can't.*

"Trust me."

I step forward, but my legs shake. "Okay." I let Dwyn adjust my direction until the tips of my toes lean over the edge. I try again to open my eyes, but the smoke stings. My legs decide they are done listening to my instructions entirely. *You can't jump, you're just a scared little girl who*— Yes I can. I can be scared, but I still have to jump.

"Jump straight down, don't go out too far," Dwyn says.

With a gulp, I reassert control over all of my rebelling appendages and step off the edge. I plummet, still holding my eyes shut. Sour air rushes into my lungs as I try to open my mouth to scream. The fall feels like an eternity, until it ends abruptly with a soft muffled thud… I'm alive?

I manage to get my eyes open, letting my adrenaline-flooded brain assess my surroundings. My sense of time returns and the eternity I spent falling is compressed into barely two seconds. I'm cradled in Dwyn's floating yellow hammock. Up above, a gaping hole is torn into the wall on the top floor, smoke pouring out like a fog machine. Out of the fog comes Dwyn, falling straight towards me.

"Watch out!" he yells.

I roll to the side, off the soft fabric and onto the hard ground. Dwyn smashes into the hammock, and it catches him like a firefighter's life net.

"I thought you weren't one for daring rescues," I say.

"I guess I did have one in me." The fire on his head shows happiness with a hint of guilt.

An alarm blares from inside the building, and the front door slams open.

"Time to go!" Dwyn says.

We run side by side away from the headquarters, towards some nearby snaking alleyways. I barely make it a few hundred feet before I fall behind. My muscles ache, my injuries sting, and my hands are still bound together. Our head start is enough that the Arbalest shouldn't know which alley we went in, but they'll catch up before long. Dwyn slows his pace to match mine, and we turn as often as possible in the labyrinthine alleys.

"So why did you come back for me?" I ask.

"I don't know," Dwyn says with a sigh.

"Thank you." I feel my lips turn to smile, but the exertion has me gasping for air, so the smile never quite comes together.

"It just seemed like the right thing to do," Dwyn mumbles.

The sound of guards disappears one at a time, until only a single set of boots thumps from behind. We turn once more down an alley, empty except for a dumpster to the left. "I can't run much more. We need to find a place to hide." Before I can even start looking, a man rounds the corner behind us. I turn to face an arbalest guard with a familiar chip on his clamshell.

"Hey! Lazzy," I shout, trying to point my shackled hands at the guard's head. "Sorry about the whole atowodite thing."

"That's the last time you make a fool out of me! Do you know how long it'll take before I can go out in the rain again with this?" Laz shouts, gesturing to the gap on his shell before pointing his gauntlet directly at me.

"Atowodite thing?" Dwyn asks.

"Not now, I'll explain later!" I drop to the ground to avoid the gauntlet's beam.

The superheated laser strikes the quartz wall to the right. Magma pours off from the wall into the alley, and I roll to the left to avoid getting burned.

"Follow my lead!" I squeeze behind the plastic dumpster.

Dwyn hesitates before doing the same. I rotate my body, pressing my knees against the wall and my back against the dumpster. Dwyn copies the movement, and together we push as hard as we can, toppling the dumpster and pouring its contents onto the ground. A pile of garbage topples onto the red-hot quartz and ignites instantly. The flame spreads to the rest of the trash, creating a pyre separating us from Laz. He yells before turning around, presumably looking for another route through the maze of alleys.

I start to run again along with Dwyn, but I immediately stop. I can't go anymore. My stomach demands food, my legs flare in pain, and my throat feels as dry as a piece of toast. Dwyn walks with me as I stumble forward. We take a few more turns before I collapse against a wall. Every alleyway in this dang place looks the same; this one even has the same dumpster. *Above it, there's a fire escape. That's your way out.*

"He'll find us," Dwyn says. "We don't have time. That one seemed to really hate you!"

I hobble to the fire escape ladder, but without my hands, I can't even get to the first rung.

"We have to go! Now!" Dwyn says.

In the distance, the sound of boots stomping gets louder and louder.

"You climb! Just gimme a sec," I say.

Dwyn quickly hops onto the dumpster and scrambles up the ladder. Standing here makes me an easy target. *Think, Lora, think.* I look over the dumpster carefully, not finding what I need. I close my eyes and focus on my sense of smell. Sorting through all the foul smells, I find it, one particularly sour scent.

Following my nose, I find a small pool of liquid at the corner of the dumpster: leftover sting rain. The tiny puddle is about twice the size of my thumb, but it should be enough. . It all makes sense now; everything is plastic or stone here because it resists acid. But not everything can be made from rock. I lower the edge of the shackles into the collected drops of acid, and smoke pours off the bonds. A quiet, high-pitched sound sizzles while the acid weakens the metal. I soak the cuffs as long as I dare, with those footsteps echoing so close. I pull out the shackles and slam them into the quartz wall, causing them to shatter. Dang, that must've looked cool!

My arms and legs cry out in pain as I scramble up the fire escape as fast as I can. At the top, Dwyn waits, hand outstretched to help me to the roof. He pulls me over a ledge surrounding the rooftop. The sound of heavy footsteps rings out from below, right as I get out of sight. As the feeling of safety washes over me, I collapse to the cold quartz ground.

The stone roof has a brim covering the perimeter with small identical holes drilled through, and the roof is slanted to draw sting rain to the edges of the building and out through the holes. However, in the clear skies, the slanted edge makes a perfect lounge chair. The cool quartz even soothes my aching muscles.

"Y'know, you really do make a good distraction," Dwyn snarks.

"Huh?"

He pulls out a small pouch brimming with glowing pink crystals. "Check it out!"

"You got the crystals back!" I say, though I find it hard to be enthusiastic.

"While the whole city was looking for you, it was easy to sneak back into Saeth," Dwyn says.

"Nice going, man. You must be happy." Doesn't he know I don't care about stupid crystals?

"You know how valuable these crystals are?"

"Yeah, you told me earlier."

"They are so valuable because they are used for fuel," Dwyn says, handing me the bag.

I let out a gasp. "For me?" I sit up, despite how comfortable my quartz chair is. "But you worked so hard to get these."

"You should be pretty close to the ship now. From here, we can go our separate ways."

"Thank you! Thank you so much!" I move to hug Dwyn. Before he even reacts, I wrap my arms around him and squeeze tightly.

"Really, really, it's nothing," Dwyn says with embarrassment while scrambling away from the embrace.

An awkward silence passes over us while we watch Naibrillar's two moons rise slowly over the horizon, giving the city's fog a pale glow.

"He could've stayed," Dwyn says, breaking the silence.

"What?" I ask.

"My dad, you're right. He could've stayed. I … wish… I mean, I would've preferred if he stayed. I thought I should tell you."

"Thank you." I smile for a moment. The movement in the blue lights above his head shows all the longing that didn't make it into words. "I can't say I know how you feel, since it hasn't been as long, but it hurts being separated from everyone I know." I take out my phone.

### 4:51 p.m., May 6th, No Service, 21% battery.

I'm probably an official missing person now, back of milk cartons and everything … I don't think I've ever seen a missing kid milk carton, now that I think about it.

I know I shouldn't use my phone. Once it dies, it's not coming back. And even if it does, without any service, it won't know what time it is back home. Even still, I need this right now. I pull up my photo app and swipe through recent pictures, most of which are of Button standing on just about every piece of furniture in the house. Between the flood of cat photos are a few pictures of my parents: Mom helping set up the festival booth last weekend, Dad rolling out dough with a rolling pin for a new recipe, the three of us on summer vacation in front of a raft of sea otters at the aquarium. "I miss them so much."

"You'll find a way to get home," comforts Dwyn.

Looking at these pictures, a soup of emotions stirs inside of me. Each feeling begging to be put into words, to finally escape my chest. They get caught in my throat, but with a deep breath, I set all my thoughts and planning aside and let my heart talk. "The last thing I said to my mom was, 'Um … thanks for the ride.' I couldn't even tell her how I feel about Evelyn, I couldn't tell anyone, and I don't even know why!" I stammer, holding back tears. "Now what if I never have the chance?" *No crying, not yet. There's still more to do.*

"You'll see your mom again, and then you can tell her whatever you want."

"I wish I would at least know how Evelyn feels about me. You've seen how much I have to know things."

"I've noticed," Dwyn says.

"I'm her best friend, so I know she loves me, but is there more? I have to know. Either way, I need my friend back. She's always been there, and now, she's just… not." My hands start to feel cold and hollow.

"Do you really think she's still…" Dwyn starts.

"She's alive." A moment of quiet passes while my assertion hangs in the air. I will save her, and I'll do it in time.

"Tell me about her," Dwyn says, lightening the mood. "Maybe I'll meet her one day."

A smile splashes onto my face with no chance of going away. I scoot right next to Dwyn as a burst of life I didn't even know I had left fills my head and heart. I pull out my phone and quickly find a picture of Evelyn from a field trip.

"There's so much, I don't know where to start," I say, practically singing. "Back home we were inseparable, friends since we were toddlers."

Dwyn nods, focusing more on me than on the picture in front of him. Though I can't take my eyes off the image of Evelyn on my screen.

"About a month ago, I was working on a project on my own. I was building a little remote-controlled car out of a shoebox and a few tiny motors. It was nothing special, but it was the first thing I finished all on my own without any help. I was so proud of that little box with unstable wheels." I pause to close my eyes and really feel like I'm back in that moment. "I didn't tell anyone, especially my mom, cause I knew she'd butt in with how to do it 'right.' But when it was done, the first thing I thought was, 'I gotta show Evelyn,'" I feel my voice wobbling. "I built the dang thing to show my mom I could do it on my own, but that feeling when I saw it drive for the first time, I wanted to share that feeling with Evelyn more

4:51pm May 6th          No Service .ull 21%

than anything." My cheeks grow warm. *You're sharing too much.* I look at Dwyn, and though his face shows no expression, I can tell he's listening.

"Go on," Dwyn says.

I hesitate before continuing. "So, I called her right away, said she had to see what I made. When she was on her way, I suddenly got so nervous. *What if she doesn't like it? Or thinks it's lame,* I kept telling myself. I was just about to text her not to come when she got there."

"Are those kinds of thoughts a human thing? Or a you thing?" Dwyn asks.

"I don't know...I think maybe a little of both." I look up at the sky, feeling the Naibrillar air on my cheeks.

"Well...what did she say?"

I smile as I hop right back to the story. "She was amazed, actually amazed at something *I* built. She asked how I did it and loved seeing it go. She even asked to paint it. She gave it this bright green and blue coat of paint. It went from looking like a dirty old shoebox to a real racecar. Then she came up with ideas for a course we could build with ramps and obstacles, sketched it out right there, and we built it together that day. I don't even remember if I ever told my parents about that car. It didn't matter." I smile the widest I've smiled since leaving Earth. Another silence falls over us, this one much more serene. For the first time in a long while, no voices intrude in my head, forcing me to keep moving or obsess over exits.

"You're right," Dwyn says.

"About?" I ask.

"She's alive."

# CHAPTER 13

# TO BOLDLY GO

Help me.[1] Help me.[2] Help me.[3] Help me.[4] Help me.[5]

♦♦♦

THE CHILLY WINDS HOWL ATOP THE SHADOW-GRAY ROOFTOP. A pale glow from Naibrillar's moons mixes with bright expressive light from below. The fresh air returns a small portion of my strength and energy. I stand up, ready for the final stretch to make it back to the ship. Dwyn remains sitting as I start towards the fire escape.

"Come with me," I say, turning back to him.

"What?"

"I'm looking for Evelyn, you're looking for your dad, and neither of us have any leads."

"So? After what happened at Saeth, I figured you'd want nothing to do with me."

"In one of my favorite books, they say 'Looking ahead is far more constructive than looking behind.' Anyways, Evelyn has to be close by, but I don't know where, so I'm looking everywhere until I have a clue. Seems like that's the only way you're finding your dad, so we might as well do it together!"

Dwyn pauses. The fire atop his head moves slowly before becoming increasingly more excited.

"Are you in or not?" I ask.

After a moment, Dwyn nods. "I'm in. I have no idea why, but I'm in."

I reach out to help him up, and we stand together atop the cold roof as the moons climb higher and higher, shimmering upon the entire city.

"We'll find them both," I say. The neon lights that fill the city give our little rooftop a warm glow as we start back to the ship.

"Lead the way," Dwyn says.

I look down the fire escape ladder. No clamshell heads in sight. "Okay. First we have to go to Fais," I say.

"What?"

"You had a deal with her. We're gonna follow through on it."

"Or we can just go straight back to the ship." I can read the objection in the flame on Dwyn's head.

"I'm scared of her too," I say. "But I don't like the idea of an angry cloud chasing us through the galaxy. So let's do the right thing."

This seems to calm Dwyn's blue fire as he follows me down the ladder. Once we are off the roof, we walk side-by-side towards Fais' hideout. It's not far, but I do not want to see another clamshell for the rest of my life, so I move carefully. Though not as carefully as

Dwyn. No matter how fast we go, he manages to make almost no sound. I have to learn how to do that. Step one: copy how he moves. I crouch down and try to match his rhythm. It's awkward at first, and I'm nowhere near as quiet, but it just feels safer to move this way.

Before long, I'm staring at the rusted dark plastic door of Fais' hideout once again. Dwyn hesitates before knocking twice. The door doesn't open. He repeats the double knock, but still the door remains shut.

"Not here," Dwyn says.

I try to push open the door, but it doesn't budge. "We should leave them for her when she gets back. Is there another way in?"

"No," Dwyn states. But then he thinks for a moment, indicated by the thoughtful way the fire dances above him. "Follow me."

At the side of the building, Dwyn feels along the smooth quartz wall and stops. He feels towards the floor until stopping his finger at a point a few inches off the ground against the wall. He flicks on his knife and presses it to the quartz. Slowly, the black stone begins to turn red and liquify as Dwyn holds his knife in place. Maybe I shouldn't think of it as a knife exactly. It's more like a blowtorch.

With careful precision, Dwyn melts away a small section of the wall to reveal thick cables. He prepares to cut them.

"Wait!" I stop him. "Sure, this will open the door, but wouldn't she be mad if we break her stuff?"

"Well…I can solder the wire back after," Dwyn says. With a quick swipe, he severs the wire, and a loud click sounds from around the corner.

Back in the workshop that smells like batteries, we find no sign of any clouds, talking or otherwise.

"See, she's gone," Dwyn says.

"You think she's out there right now looking for us?"

"Probably." Dwyn pulls out a few of the crystals from his satchel. "You know these are fuel right? Each one we give her is less distance we can get on that ship."

"I know, but it's the right thing to do. Besides, Evelyn can't be far, and I'm sure we'll find your dad along the way." Reluctantly, Dwyn places a handful of the crystals on Fais' desk before leaving. He quickly fixes the wire, and I test to make sure the door is locked once again.

On our way back to the ship, I keep trying to emulate Dwyn's form by stepping with long horizontal strides, lifting my feet as little as possible. Still too loud, but I'm getting better. At the next alley, I stop as I spot an Arbalest guard around the corner. I copy a gesture from a spy movie I saw to signal Dwyn. He doesn't seem to get it, but he notices the guard regardless. Right, his alien senses are better than mine. We take a path to avoid the guard and get to the edge of the city.

Before long, we return to the clearing where I last left the ship, and I pull out the Sydon crystals. "Hey, ship! We got the fuel. Where does this stuff go?"

In response, a small compartment slides open in a spiral, revealing a small hexagonal tube leading inside the ship. I push the crystals in. *The tree branches are gone.* That's odd. Why are they all on the ground? Did they slip off?

"Congratulations, you managed to do a basic fuel refill," the ship states.

"It's more than you did!" I say. "All you did is sit here."

"In the hours you were gone, I solved a quintillion mathematical problems far beyond your comprehension," the ship boasts.

"Oh yeah? How many of them would've gotten us outta here?" The ship does not respond but instead opens the glass dome, giving us access to the cockpit. Dwyn climbs first, and I follow.

"You expected that I would simply let you leave?" a voice rumbles from inside the ship.

I freeze on the ladder. I look up, Dwyn blocks my view, but I know that voice.

"Fais," Dwyn says. "I can explain, we were j—"

A loud crash, like the sound of a whip, booms from above. Dwyn goes flying down the ladder and takes me with him. Dwyn orients himself quickly, but I take another moment to stand. Fais hovers menacingly above the ship ladder.

"Why didn't you tell us she was here, ship!" I yell.

"I was not instructed to keep a list of visitors during your absence."

"But you coulda—"

"Enough!" Fais interrupts. "The time to pay your debt has concluded. And you, human girl, caused quite the stir among the Arbalest. All very bad for business."

"Fais, just listen! You wanted the crystals, right? Well, we left some at your place! The amount we owe, so we should be even-steven." I try to get her to see reason. But the only response Fais gives is a bolt of lightning that strikes just next to Dwyn.

"Run!" he says.

I'm tired of running, but I suspect I would be more tired of being zapped by an alien cloud, so running it is.

After a few seconds, I stop and turn to Dwyn. "Wait. Look, she's not chasing us." I point towards the ship. Fais remains floating like a distant storm cloud, but she does not move any closer.

"Yvxywyndk!" Dwyn exclaims, making a sound I never heard before. Wait, was that word…not translated?

"What is it?"

"She was waiting for us. She knew we had the crystals and were going to try to get off the planet. She wants to take the ship!"

"No! We have to go back. We can't let her," I say. "It's my only chance to find Evelyn."

"We also can't stop her. Our only chance would be to throw the knife and hit a tiny spot inside the cloud. If I miss it'll be all over, and that's only if I avoid getting electrocuted first."

"You were pretty accurate with it before."

The flame on Dwyn's head did not like that remark. "There'll be other ships. We can figure something out."

It has to be this one. How can I explain it? "This is the one that I came here on. This is the one that was there when Evelyn was—"

"Oh no," Dwyn says.

"What now?" I look up. "Oh no."

From the direction of the city, a large figure strides towards us. Tall, strong, and wearing a hood that does not hide his black-and-white-striped face. The captain of the Arbalest walks with long methodical strides as he pulls out a large alien device. I don't recognize it, but I can tell I do not want it pointed at me. We back away slowly from the captain, towards the ship, towards Fais.

"What is he doing here?" Dwyn says. The blue flame on his head sparks with more emotion than I've seen in it before. Somehow, the fire's movements convey a spiteful anger that can only be personal.

"You know him?" I ask, still backing away.

"Rewyth is my uncle," Dwyn says. "How many Lelogs do you expect to see on a planet this far away?"

"First off, how was I supposed to know how far away Lelog is?" I begin. "And second, why didn't you say that the captain of the

Arbalest was your *uncle?*"

"Well…you didn't—"

"No, no, no. Don't give me the same excuse as the ship! And third off, how was I supposed to know you were the same species? You look nothing alike! You're pink!"

Dwyn doesn't get a chance to respond as the rumbling sound of Fais echoes much closer than I prefer. Sweat beads at my forehead as Fais floats down from the ship and hovers a few feet off the ground as normal. Rewyth approaches, still holding the same device, which begins to glow a deep red. Yup, definitely don't want that pointed at me.

"A third thief… find one, more must be scurrying close by," the captain says, aiming his gaze towards the cloud. "You must be Fais, the Novmura. I've had a team looking for you for months."

*The exit is ten feet away.* The only way off this planet is that ship. There is an evil cloud and an alien with some crazy weapon. *What can you do?* I can come up with something, I just need to—

**WOOSH!** A gust of wind bursts from Fais and collides with everyone. "Fools! You led the captain of the Arbalest here?" The wind carries Fais' words and forces me to stagger backwards. The captain manages to hold his ground, but his hood blows back, revealing a pale blue flame at the top of his head. Now I'm starting to see the resemblance.

At my side, Dwyn grips his knife handle tightly, his thumb hovering over the switch to flick it on. Fais continues to float near the ship, and the baseball-sized black sphere at her center bounces back and forth between facing me and the captain. Meanwhile, Rewyth stands a hundred feet away, forming a triangle between the three groups.

*Think, Lora. Think.* If Dwyn throws the knife at either one, we're helpless against the other. Plus if he misses, Fais will electrocute us. Except that if she does, the captain could blast her with whatever that thing he's carrying does… Does it work on clouds?

Sparks crackle lightly from Fais, as though she were preparing to launch a bolt of lightning. I tense, preparing for the worst. The blue fire above Dwyn trembles for a moment. But nothing happens; Fais' core continues to look back and forth between me, Dwyn, and the captain.

The captain looks me up and down, then Fais, then Dwyn. He spends a moment staring at the knife Dwyn holds, but he doesn't

point his weapon at anyone… yet.

Dwyn's hand moves, getting to a better position to throw. I gesture for Dwyn to wait, slow enough to not catch the attention of the others, but hopefully with enough urgency to stop Dwyn from starting an all-out attack.

She isn't zapping anyone yet. That means whatever the captain is holding is a threat. Fais is rational. She has to see the captain as a bigger danger to herself. If everyone tries to attack at the same time, she'll go for him. That just leaves one person to worry about…I hope.

I focus my attention on Dwyn's uncle, and a lump forms in my throat as I imagine all the horrible things that weapon in his hands might do to me. The flame on the captain's head, unlike Dwyn's, flows calmly with a pale blue glow. He must not be scared of Fais. Either he doesn't know how dangerous she is, or he doesn't care. But he also hasn't attacked us yet, which means he must at least respect her as a possible threat.

"Y…you," I croak, as if I forgot how to talk in the long silence. I try to continue speaking as calmly as I can. The opposite of my sci-fi-club-president voice. "You want us gone, and we're trying to leave." I watch for changes in the captain's fire, but there are none, so I continue. "You told me you hated thieves, but you were one once, right?" As I thought, the captain says nothing. Then I see it: a tiny disturbance in the flame, barely noticeable if I wasn't looking. Despite how small the change is, I can tell what that little flicker means. A moment of doubt.

Alright, he does feel something about his past. "I know you feel some guilt, and if you're not honest with yourself, life will never be honest with you." More guilt burns in the fire. *Not enough, push just a little harder.*

"We're trying to find his dad, who I assume is the brother you betrayed. Let all that remorse out!" The flame rages momentarily before calming back down, though with noticeably more ferocity. *Okay, too much.*

"What are you doing?" Dwyn whispers.

"Don't speak of such things." The captain breaks his silence. His eyes focus on me now, no longer checking Fais. Meanwhile, Fais seems to concentrate on me, but only for a few extra seconds. Then she directs all her attention at the captain. No, no, she'll see this as a chance to take out the captain. Then us…*You screwed it up.*

"Rewyth!" Dwyn shouts, stepping forward. Everyone's attention snaps to Dwyn. "You sold out my dad. He should've hated you, but he talked as if you did the right thing. He was *impressed*."

Did Dwyn figure out what I was doing? I watch the fire on the captain's head. The anger is still there, but the disturbance returns. "Enough of this!" Fais responds with her voice of distant thunder. Sparks, much bigger this time, pop from every inch of the cloud. Dwyn flicks on his knife, the red blade illuminating the side of his face. He doesn't move to attack, but the threat is clear. If Fais attacks the captain, Dwyn will go for Fais. The stalemate continues.

"What does it matter now?" Dwyn's uncle finally says. "He would've done the same to me. Everyone is out for themselves. That's just how things work."

"You're right," Dwyn replies. "He left me to—" Dwyn pauses for a second, taking another breath before continuing. "He left me so he could escape. Just like him, I told myself it was the right thing. Then I did the same to Lora."

The flicker appears again, a pattern in the fire I recognize. A pattern above both Dwyn and the captain. A pattern that means regret.

"I left her as a distraction for the same reason he left me, and the same reason you left him."

"So what?" the captain says. His voice appears confident, but the flame gives away the truth.

That's when Fais starts to make her move. Electricity flashes around her like a dozen strobe lights out of sync.

Instead of attacking with his knife, Dwyn makes one more appeal to his uncle. "I could've stayed with her, he could've stayed with me, and Rewyth, you could've stayed with him."

The captain turns and points his glowing weapon at Fais. She has no choice but to respond by attacking the bigger threat. A bolt of lightning cracks across the field at the captain as he fires a beam much like those from the gauntlets towards Fais. Dwyn takes his chance to throw his knife directly at the center of the distracted cloud.

The lightning strikes the captain's alien weapon, and it explodes, knocking him to the ground. Fais narrowly avoids the beam, but with her attention completely held by the captain, Dwyn's knife hits its mark. The blade glances the side of the black orb at Fais' center, her core. The cloud disappears, and the core falls to the ground with a thump. And all is quiet for a moment.

Dwyn and I walk over to Fais' core on the ground. A single crack runs along the side of the orb. "Is she...?" I ask.

"No, Novmuras are a lot tougher to kill than that, but she won't wake up anytime soon," Dwyn explains. I breathe a sigh of relief, which Dwyn interrupts. "I hated Fais, but she wasn't wrong."

"What do you mean?"

"Well...I owed her for the hacking device. And she had no reason to believe we left her the crystals."

"That doesn't mean she should've attacked us!"

"Maybe." Dwyn pauses to carefully pick up his knife. I spot a hint of reverence as Dwyn looks over the blade, shuts it off, and returns it to his belt. "She should recover with a new cloud in a year or two."

"At which point she'll find herself in a cell," a voice calls from behind. Rewyth stands up. "We still have an empty one we...failed to fill earlier."

Dwyn puts his hand on his knife but waits to draw as I inspect the captain's calm flame. "There's no need for that," Rewyth says.

"Does that mean you'll let us go?" I ask.

"You have caused enough trouble to warrant imprisonment for however long humans live," Rewyth explains. "But I suspect if I wish to avoid trouble, I want to keep you as far away from my planet as possible."

It sounds like a lecture the principal might give. Something like "You're causing a lot of trouble at this school." But to be called trouble for a *whole* planet? I can't help but smile.

"You said you know about Earth, right?" I ask. "Have you been there? How do you get there? Do you know who kidnapped us?"

"You ask a lot of questions," Rewyth says. *He really is Dwyn's uncle.* "I don't know much," he continues. "Years ago a man asked me if I had records about a planet called 'Earth'. The Arbalest keep good records on off-worlders, but we had nothing."

I lean forward, trying to absorb every last detail of the story. It may not be all the answers I need, but after all this time, at least I'm getting a clue.

"I tried to question the man further, but he fled. I sent a dozen of my best after him, but he escaped."

"Not that I'm complaining, but your guards do have pretty bad aim," I say.

"We're working on that," Rewyth replies. "I don't know what

he wanted, but I checked the logs, and the only ship to leave our atmosphere that day was headed towards Buscura."

"Buscura?" I ask.

"Buscura," Dwyn scoffs.

"What's Buscura?"

"It's a planet a few systems deeper into Taith," the captain explains.

"What's—" I start, but Dwyn interrupts before I even ask my question.

"Taith is this section of the galaxy." I silently thank Dwyn for the answer as he continues. "As for Buscura, my dad used to talk about that planet all the time. The richest people in the galaxy live there, plenty to steal."

"He told you about that plan too?" Rewyth asked. "It was just about the most foolish plan I ever came up with."

"That came from you?" Dwyn asks.

"It was a long time ago."

"Wait," I interject. "Do you think your dad might be there too?"

"Maybe," he replies. "We'll see."

"You're going too?" Rewyth asks.

"I'm going to find him," Dwyn states.

The captain stands in silence for a time, then simply says, "Good."

Dwyn stares at his uncle for another silent moment before turning towards the ship, and I move to follow.

"Lora," the captain starts.

I turn to him.

"I hope you find her," the captain says, struggling as though the words didn't belong in his mouth.

"I will."

I hop into the ship, and Dwyn does the same. The glass dome closes over us.

"Hey, ship, how do I fly you?" I ask.

"I would explain, but I doubt it'll be much help. I'll light up the buttons to trigger autopilot. I assume you can manage that," the ship states dryly.

"What's your problem!" Dwyn shouts at the ship.

"I have no problems," the ship responds.

A button lights up, and I slam it with my palm. The ship begins to hum and vibrate. Small lights guide me to flick a switch with a satisfying tactile click. Oh, my god, I'm flying a spaceship! I don't even have a driver's license.

"Set course for Buscura!" We start to lift off from Naibrillar slowly, and the ship orients itself towards a large star in the distance. "So… Dwyn? Why did Rewyth say the plan to go to this planet was 'foolish'?"

"You think everyone in this galaxy is as gullible and slow as the Arbalest? You said it yourself, bad aim."

"Um… you make it sound like we didn't almost die like fifty times over."

"Well… I only count four."

"Please tell me this is one of those jokes you said you had in space." He doesn't respond, but seeing the way the fire moves above his head tells me all I need to know. I take a deep breath and continue to follow the ship's flight instructions. There are so many buttons it sometimes takes minutes just to find which one is lit up.

After a while, Dwyn speaks again. "You really think Evelyn's there?"

"She has to be." I check the time on my phone.

### 7:09 p.m., May 6th, No Service, 17% battery.

Only eleven days to the dance. It's going to be fine. In two weeks, we'll just be able to laugh about all this. I slide the phone back to my pocket and ready myself to head into the stars. I press another glowing button, and the ship accelerates dramatically. The sudden force flings me to the ground. Once the inertia balances out, I look up from the floor. Wedged underneath a seat is a small green bag.

"No way!" I pull it loose.

"What's that?" Dwyn asks.

"It's my backpack! I guess I was still wearing it when I got here. It must've fallen off during the crash." I sit down, unzip it, and reach inside. First I find my portable charger. Finally! I didn't see a single outlet that works with my phone this entire time.

Next, I find the sketch of Captain Jacques P. Killian. The moment I see the confidence in his expression, I start to laugh before digging into my backpack.

"Hey, what is that?" Dwyn asks.

"No way!" I drop everything in my hands and pull out the most beautiful thing I have ever seen. A sealed Tupperware container holding three pork dumplings. I rip the lid off and inhale the first two. I never thought three-day-old dumplings could be so good! *You're gonna get sick.* I don't care.

I look over at Dwyn, whose flame dances quizzically atop his head. Then I look at the sole remaining dumpling, then back at Dwyn, then back to my dumpling. Dang it. I sigh and stretch out my arm to him. "You gotta try this. This is what food is supposed to taste like."

Dwyn cautiously reaches out and takes the dumpling. He gently squishes it slightly to assess the texture. He takes a bite, looking around quickly as he chews.

"You like it?" He better like it. If I waste my last dumpling on someone who doesn't appreciate it…

"Tastes weird," Dwyn says.

"Excuse me! You gave me the nastiest food in the universe, and all you have to say about this is 'tastes weird'?" I *try* to appreciate the fact that I'm the first human to make the discovery that alien tastebuds suck. If only I didn't have to sacrifice the best food in the whole galaxy to find that out.

I check my backpack again to see if I missed anything, and a small neon-green golf ball falls to the ground. I crouch to pick it up, but then something catches my eye. The drawing of Captain Jacques P. Killian has a letter written on the back.

Dear Lora,

There's so much I want to say, so much more than I can fit on the back of some nerd drawing. It sucks that I have to move, I know that you know it sucks, but I still want to say it. Have it in writing, so no one can ever pretend I'm ok with all this. I'll miss so many things, ~~like going over to your~~

Official list of things I will miss:

1. Going over to your place for dinner. There's 8 million people in Voigt City, and I bet none are as good of a cook as your dad.

2. Getting to make improvements to Cecilia. (I named the car Cecilia, I hope you don't mind.)

3. Seeing you take up the entirety of Mr. Aledy's class going off about your newest sci-fi book. (I counted four times that saved me from turning in an assignment.)

4. Our spot at lunch that maybe only 10 people in the whole school know about.

5.

Ok, maybe listing these things wasn't a good idea, I'm totally running out of space. What I wanted to say is that you're the one I'm really going to miss. I mean, when things were tough, like with my parents. ~~And I needed~~ You were just always there for me, and I wanted to ~~say it~~ write it.

Love, Evelyn.

With trembling hands, I return the picture to my bag. I pick up the golf ball with two fingers and hold it out towards the window, making it look like a planet among the panorama of stars around me. She is orbiting around one of those billion dots out there. It might seem impossible, but I don't care. I'm not done.

*Wherever you are, I'll find you.*

THE

END

# THANK YOU

I appreciate that you have taken the time to read the first Worlds Apart book, and I hope you enjoyed this story at least half as much as a I enjoyed telling it. If you want to stay up to date with Lora's adventures or see what other stories I am cooking up, feel free to join my mailing list. You can find it at **www.ianfanselow.com** along with a form to contact me if needed.
Additionally, if you have the time to leave a review on Amazon it would help me immensely. Not just because of the numbers, but also because I want to know what your experience with Lora's adventure was like!
Finally, if there are people in your life that you feel may connect with this story and its characters, please share it with them.

More adventures to come,

Ian Fanselow

# PUZZLES



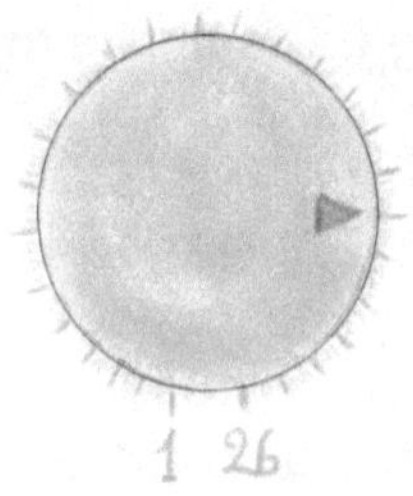


12,31,38,15,59     86,1,61,44     45,105,64,41,14

6:12     12:31     4:21
2:24     4:65     13:33
1:55     10:53

42/25/2   15/5/9   111/9/3   18/1/12   17/19/3
28/15/2   62/6/3   78/9/10   4/11/06   52/5/11
65/7/4   109/5/5   20/11/5   29/2/12   84/10/4
98/1/3   35/14/5   68/5/10

# PUZZLES

If you try, I'm not so hard to find.
I'm in so many places, perhaps even nine.
The picture you'll see is mine.
But what are the names for each of these times?

# PRONUNCIATION GUIDE

If you find yourself arguing about the "correct" way to say any of the names in this book, look no further than this handy dandy pronunciation guide.

**Lora:** rhymes with "Flora"

**Harthian:** Sounds like "Hearth" rhyming with "Darth" followed by "Ian" (Hey, that's my name!)

**Dwyn:** Rhymes with "Win" combine the name "Dwayne" with the word "Win"

**Lelog:** "Lee" plus "log"

**Glyf:** Same pronunciation as "Glyph". Rhymes with "Whiff"

**Elicyf:** sounds like "Ele" as in the first part of the word "Element" then "cyf" also rhymes with "Whiff"

**Saeth:** rhymes with "eighth"

**Taith:** rhymes with "Saeth"

**Fais:** rhymes with "rice"

**Naibrillar:** sounds like "nigh" which rhymes with "lie" followed by "brill" which rhymes with "drill" then "ar" like the sound a pirate makes.

**Rewyth:** Sounds like if you were about to say the word "red" but changed your mind halfway through and then said "with"

**Laz:** rhymes with "has"

**Buscura:** the first part "bu" rhymes with "boo" the sound a ghost makes. followed by "scura" which would rhyme with "cure + uh"

**Fydlon:** "fyd" rhymes with "lid" followed by "lon" which sounds like the first part of "London"

**Arwein:** "ar" like "are" or the sound a pirate makes. Followed by "wein" which sounds like "wane"